The Rogue

A HIGHLAND GUARD NOVELLA

OTHER BOOKS BY MONICA

New York Times & USA Today Bestselling Author

MONICA McCARTY

The Rogue

A HIGHLAND GUARD NOVELLA

DEDICATION

To my daughter, Maxine, who is now old enough to appreciate this cover.

ACKNOWLEDGMENTS

A huge thanks to Jami Alden for reading this so quickly and for being the greatest beta reader ever. Thanks also to Carrie at Seductive Designs for the gorgeous cover, Ellie at Love N. Books for helping to facilitate the great photo for the cover, and the amazing Stuart Reardon—a model I'd be happy to have on any of my books. On the production side, a huge thanks to Shona McCarthy for her always excellent copyediting, Anne Victory and Crystalle for their eagle-eyed "oops" detecting, Lisa Rogers for the e-book formatting, and Isobel Carr for the print formatting.

.

CHAPTER ONE

Edinburgh, Scotland, March 1314

HOW SHE WAS GOING TO PAY her cousin back for this was all Isabel Stewart could think of as she rode away from Holyrood Abbey beside Sir Too-Good-To-Be-True. Good gracious, an hour—God forbid *two*—of listening to whatever puffery Sir Thomas Randolph thought she wanted to hear was too much to be borne, even in the name of friendship.

Not that the esteemed knight looked very interested in charming or impressing her at the moment. A covert glance from under her lashes at her distinctly grim-looking companion told her that he wasn't any happier being forced into her company than she was his. The try-not-to-fall-in-love-with-me grin that was perpetually plastered on his face was nowhere to be seen.

Dislike was probably too strong of a word for it, but when Izzie arrived in Edinburgh four days ago and met the man her cousin hoped to marry, he and Izzie hadn't exactly taken to one another. It was probably Izzie's fault. She hadn't been able to hide her amusement at his grandiose greeting. But good grief, she'd felt as though she was watching a player upon a stage act out the most perfect, romantic fantasy of the handsome knight in shining armor riding in on his magnificent charger and kneeling before his lady fair. It had been too much to take.

Clearly, Randolph (despite his new title of Earl of

Moray, everyone called him Randolph) hadn't seen the humor in the situation and had taken definite umbrage at her reaction—if that rigid back, stony jaw, and icy gaze meant anything. He might be perfect, and she had to admit his face came exceedingly close, but he seemed to know it and took himself far too seriously for her liking.

Which was ironic since in the four days that she'd known him, she doubted she'd heard one real thought come out of his mouth. He had a distinct knack for saying just the right thing—or rather what he thought you wanted to hear—which was undeniably charming, but again made her feel as though she was watching a performance. A magnificent performance without a doubt, but a performance all the same.

Still, there was something undeniably captivating about his larger-than-life personality and brash arrogance, and just like everyone else, she couldn't help watching him. Sir Thomas Randolph was a great hero in the making—a man who would become legend—and everyone knew it.

So why was Randolph taking Izzie to see the rock formations known as Samson's Ribs in the park next to Holyrood Abbey, and not her cousin Elizabeth, to whom he was all but engaged? Good question! And one Izzie intended to have her cousin answer as soon as she returned.

Izzie suspected it had something to do with Elizabeth's handsome childhood friend, Thom MacGowan. But her cousin better figure out which of the two Thomases she wanted—preferably before Izzie had to cover for her again. One uncomfortable ride through the park was more than enough.

At least they weren't alone, although it felt like it. As the favored nephew of King Robert the Bruce, Sir Thomas Randolph was one of the most important, wealthiest men in the kingdom, and the retinue of men around him reflected that. Though there were probably three score of men-at-arms in his service, only a handful had accompanied them today. The men, however, were riding at a discreet distance behind them.

Apparently, they hadn't been informed of the change in plans, she thought with a wry smile. It was no longer the romantic ride and midday meal in a basket that Sir Thomas had intended with her cousin. Still, Izzie had no doubt that most of the women at court—including many of the married ones—would give their eyeteeth to be in her position. And she would gladly switch positions with any one of them. The awkward silence was unbearable.

But what could they talk about? They didn't have anything in common. She frowned. Except for music. She wasn't surprised that he sang—what self-respecting knight in shining armor couldn't sing a chanson de geste about some chivalrous tale?—rather, she'd been surprised by the depth of his skill and the attention he'd obviously given to the study.

It seemed a safe enough place to start. They had to talk about *something,* for goodness sake. And preferably something that wasn't going to make his spine stiffen and that formidable jaw of his turn to stone, which she seemed to have a unique ability to do every time she opened her mouth. She wasn't purposefully trying to antagonize him; it just sort of happened.

With a heavy sigh, she looked over at him. She would have blinked a few times, but from experience she knew it wouldn't dull the effect any. He really was startlingly magnificent to look at—the dark, glossy hair, the brilliant hazel eyes that sometimes looked green, and the refined, arrogantly handsome features that were it not for the strong jaw, once-broken nose, a few thin battle-scars, and fiercely proud expression on his face, might have verged on prettiness. He was built rather magnificently as well, with the broad shoulders and the powerful chest and muscular arms of a man who'd probably had a sword in his hand since he could walk. But it was his mouth that undoubtedly made women lose their heads. It was pure sin with a sensual twist—when it wasn't pressed into a thin line around her, that is.

Simply gorgeous, she thought to herself in the same way

that one might admire a fine jewel or decorative artwork—from afar. It certainly wasn't something she wanted for herself. Her cousin Elizabeth would have her hands full with him. From what she heard, Sir Thomas was a very popular man at court with the ladies. They loved him.

It wasn't hard to see why. "What's not to love?" her cousin liked to jest. He was rich, handsome, and charming. Seemingly too good to be true. Which in Izzie's experience meant that he likely was. Despite his surface charm and gallantry, she sensed something cold underneath—as if emotion was something Randolph might play at as well. He could put on a good show, but she wagered very little really touched him.

"Look," she said now, trying to hide her amusement. The situation was ridiculous, but she knew better than to think that he would see the humor. "I know this isn't the day either of us had planned, but we might as well make the best of it. I'm sure we can find *something* to talk about to pass the time." She was aware that she didn't actually sound too sure, which, if the arch of his brow meant anything, he seemed to be aware of as well. "Perhaps you might tell me about your musical training," she added hastily, recalling the surprisingly passionate exchange they'd had about music the other day. "Where did you learn to sing like that? You had the nuns spellbound yesterday."

He held her gaze a little too long, as if he were trying to figure out some ulterior meaning to her words. Eventually he let the brow drop. It was a bit like lowering a shield. "Only the nuns, Lady Isabel?"

She tried not to flush, knowing full well that he might have caught her staring once or twice. But she was stunned, not mesmerized—there was a difference. Pretending she didn't know to what he was referring, she said, "Perhaps a few of the patients as well."

She sobered. There had been one young girl in particular—probably no older then fourteen—who had looked at him as if he were an angel descended from the very heavens that would be claiming her soon. He'd been the perfect, gallant knight, sitting by her bed and making her laugh with his stories—much to the admiration of everyone around. Izzie couldn't help but wonder whether that was why he'd done it. She sensed that appearances mattered to Sir Thomas Randolph. He was one of the greatest knights in the kingdom and everyone had to see it.

Their eyes met for an instant, and from the shadow that crossed his face, she wondered if he were remembering the girl, too. But that wasn't likely. There were few noblemen who would trouble themselves with a poor, dying peasant girl, and certainly not ones who had been charged by the king with the difficult task of taking Edinburgh Castle from the English. Randolph was so busy commanding the siege of the important castle, he barely had time for the woman he was supposed to be courting for marriage.

Not that her cousin was any better. Elizabeth's head was so turned by the handsome Thom MacGowan that so far Izzie had ended up talking to Randolph more than her cousin had.

Apparently, thinking that he'd made his point, which in a way she conceded he had, he let the matter of catching her staring drop. "The village school attached to the church where I grew up," he said, answering her original question. "In addition to Latin grammar, the priest also instructed us in music. I proved a far more proficient student at the latter."

She grinned, feigning shock. "Do you mean there is actually something in which you do not excel, my lord?"

The words were out before she could take them back. Anyone else would have heard them for the teasing jest that they were. But Sir Thomas Randolph was deaf to teasing—and humor.

His face darkened, and she saw the telltale tic appear at his jaw.

Oh no, she'd done it again.

She sighed. Oh well. So much for finding something safe to talk about.

❧

RANDOLPH STARED AT THE WOMAN riding beside him and tried to contain his irritation. But if he were a dog, his hackles would be rising. Hell, they'd be standing all the way on end.

What was it about Lady Isabel Stewart that made him feel as if a nettle had worked its way under his plaid and wouldn't stop poking? There was nothing outwardly in her appearance to give an indication of trouble. Fair-haired and blue-eyed, with pretty enough, finely boned features, she was so serene-looking her likeness would not have seemed out of place on a church wall.

Too bad her temperament didn't match.

From the first moment they'd met, he sensed that she was amused by him—and not in the way he was used to amusing women. Nay, it was almost as if she was laughing *at* him. Which was ridiculous. Women didn't laugh at him. They smiled, flirted, and occasionally simpered, but they definitely didn't laugh. They might bat their eyes, but they sure as hell didn't roll them, as he could swear he'd seen her do more than once.

What the Devil was wrong with the lass?

She didn't even look at him the way other women did. He hadn't noticed the difference until meeting her had made it clear. *Un*awareness. That's what it was, and he didn't like it. Especially as he could hardly make the same claim toward her. He was oddly attracted to her, which under the circumstances, only increased his annoyance. He was about to ask her extremely beautiful and would-make-him-a-perfect-wife cousin to marry him, for Christ's sake. He shouldn't be thinking of ways to make Isabel—"Izzie" as her family called her—aware of him. Plenty of women were aware of him; he didn't need another.

But it didn't stop him from imagining how satisfying it would be to see those big, laughing blue eyes darken with arousal and those pink lips, always set in a wry grin, part with a gasp of pleasure.

It wasn't just her unawareness riling his irritation this time, however. Unknowingly she'd struck a tender spot. Learning hadn't come easy to him. "Not all of us are born to be clerks or churchmen." With a long, meaningful look, he couldn't resist adding, "Indeed there are other things in which I do excel that ensure priesthood will never be in my future."

When she took his meaning, he was rewarded with a sharp intake of breath that if not a hint of passion, was close enough for him to imagine it could be. Viscerally. He felt it run through him in a hot buzz as if a lightning bolt had been set at the base of his spine.

Their eyes met, and in her shock, he wondered if maybe she wasn't quite as unaware as he thought.

But just as he was about chastise himself for acting like an arse by baiting her—inappropriately—to salve his pride, she did it again. She laughed and gave a half roll of her eyes. "So I've heard."

Damn her. At least if she were haughty, condescending, or judgmental, he'd have cause to be so irritated. But it was partly the good humor with which she imparted her indifference that annoyed him. She might have been a distant aunt, teasing him for being incorrigible.

But she wasn't his aunt, damn it. She was the twenty-two-year-old unmarried daughter of the great patriot hero John Stewart of Bonkyll, who'd died leading his archers beside William Wallace at Falkirk sixteen years ago. She was also cousin to both the Lord of Douglas and the current Steward of Scotland. In other words, she was just the kind of well-connected young noblewoman who usually tried to impress *him*.

But she didn't seem to care what he thought, and he knew it wasn't because he was nearly engaged to her cousin. Nay, she'd simply sized him up and found him somehow wanting. *Him.* Wanting! And that irritated him to no end.

She was a young woman at court for the first time, and he was one of the most important knights in the kingdom. It was unnatural, blast it.

What did he need to do to impress her, slay a dragon? Hell, that probably wouldn't even do it. She was remarkably *un*impressible.

Why the hell was he even thinking about this? It was probably the novelty of having a young woman not interested in him. Aye, that must be it.

Still, he couldn't resist prodding her a little. "I'd tell you not to believe everything you hear, but in this case..." He shrugged with a wicked smile.

To which she was completely immune. His comment merely elicited another eye roll and an adorably twitching mouth. "I'm sure everything you do is perfect, my lord."

He pulled on the reins, and swung around his horse to face her. "What the Devil is that supposed to mean?"

She didn't seem taken aback by his anger at all. Rather the opposite as a matter of fact. The lass was entirely too self-possessed for one so young. It was disconcerting, and he didn't like it.

She stopped her own horse and turned to face him, shaking her head with a wry smile and something of an "Are you kidding me?" expression on her face. "Come now, my lord, is that not what I'm supposed to think? Sir Thomas Randolph, the perfect, quintessential knight: handsome, charming, chivalrous to the core, whose prowess on the battlefield is only equaled by his prowess in the bedchamber?"

Randolph's mouth might have gaped. She'd shocked him speechless. Now, admittedly he'd been suggesting that very thing, but for her to come out and actually say it was different. It made him feel almost... embarrassed. Hell, he *was* embarrassed.

How did she do this, damn it? How did she so easily turn the tables on him when he was the aggrieved party? Wasn't he?

Bloody hell.

He would have dragged his fingers through his hair if he wasn't wearing a helm. "It isn't like that."

She smiled, clearly amused. "Isn't it? But no matter, my lord. I did not mean to offend you. I think it's just that we don't share the same sense of humor."

That was an understatement.

She tilted her head, her mouth in a bit of a frown. "Do you ever laugh, my lord?"

"Of course." All the women found him quite witty. All except her, that is. He laughed with them... didn't he?

Her mouth twitched again, and he knew she was fighting a smile. He suspected because he'd been scowling as he answered. "I should like to see it."

His scowl deepened. She had an uncanny way of making him feel defensive. "Perhaps you might try by saying something that was actually funny."

The words were out before he could stop them. It was a rude and ungallant thing to say. He was *never* rude and ungallant—especially to a young lady.

But if he was worried about offending her, he should have known better.

She looked over at him, clearly startled, and then did something extraordinary. She burst out into laughter. Deep, honest-to-God, joyous laughter. It was beautiful to hear— even more so than her singing the day before, which had conjured images of angels and other heavenly creatures.

"I suppose I deserved that," she said with her typical good-natured wryness. She tilted her head, studying him with an intensity that made him vaguely uncomfortable. "You should be forthcoming more often, my lord. It becomes you."

"I'll try to remember that." He gave her an odd look. He didn't know what the hell to make of her, and it showed. "You are an unusual young woman, Lady Isabel."

Proving the truth of his comment, she beamed. "Thank you. I think that is the nicest thing you have ever said to me."

He hadn't necessarily meant it as a compliment.

She laughed again, demonstrating a disconcerting ability to read his thoughts. "Even if you hadn't meant it as a compliment." When he reflexively started to assure her otherwise, she stopped him. "No pretty protests, please. Do not ruin the good impression left by your honesty. Perhaps you can think of something else rude to say instead?"

Her eyes sparkled with amusement. They were the prettiest shade of light blue—like the sun on a crystal clear spring day. A day much like today as a matter of fact.

Randolph was pretty sure this was the oddest conversation he'd ever had. "Give me a minute or two. I'm sure you'll make me think of something."

She laughed again. "Keep this up, my lord, and you will have me swooning at your feet."

I'd pay to see that.

He didn't realize he'd muttered it aloud until she gave a fresh burst of laughter. "Why, when there are so many willing to do so for free?"

Their eyes met. Was she teasing him or laughing at him again? He couldn't tell. That was part of the problem.

Suspecting that if he tried to continue the conversation, she'd keep getting the last word, he did something rare and gave up.

They rode for a few minutes in companionable silence until he heard her gasp.

"Is that it?" she asked, pointing to the hill and cliffs that had just appeared before them.

"Aye. The hill is known as Arthur's Seat, and those oddly shaped columns of rock in the cliffs on the southwest side are Samson's Ribs."

Her eyes lit with excitement, and it hit him with the force of a hammer. Low in his gut at first, then stirring rather hard below his belt.

Christ, she should look like that all the time. Animated and full of excitement, she was about as far from serene as he could imagine. She was lovely... absolutely breathtaking.

"They are magnificent! I've never seen cliffs shaped like that. And they are aptly named, indeed; the square sided columns look like ribs."

"Hexagonal," he corrected automatically. "When you get up close you can see the six sides of the columns. There are similar rocks on the Isle of Staffa and along the coast of Northern Ireland."

"There are?" She was honestly amazed, and for the first time he felt as if he might have impressed her with something. He liked the feeling. He liked it a lot.

"Can we get closer?" she asked.

"If you'd like."

The words were barely out of his mouth before she snapped her reins and raced off ahead.

Strangely caught up in her enthusiasm, he told his men to wait there for them and set up their meal while he rode after her.

She was a good rider, he noticed, but that didn't surprise him. She seemed the kind of woman who would be just as comfortable roaming the moors as she would be sitting on the dais in the Great Hall of some fine castle. There was a genuineness to her, a lack of pretense that made her seem grounded in whatever she seemed to be doing.

She was already tying her reins to a tree when he caught up to her.

He dismounted, tied up his own horse, and followed after her along the narrow path that circled the base of the rock.

She seemed to dance through the ankle-high grass, still brown from winter, as she walked. If he wasn't so acutely aware of the shapely hips, round bottom, and very womanly chest revealed quite splendidly in her form-fitting, green wool gown, he might have thought he was watching a child let out of doors for the first time after a long, cold winter.

The thought made him smile, which he was still doing when she reached the furthermost curve and turned to look at him.

She seemed startled. He could have sworn he heard a sharp intake of breath, and the pulse at her neck appeared to flutter a little faster.

"Is something wrong?" he asked.

She blinked a few times and shook her head. "You've

never smiled like that before."

He frowned. "Like what?"

But she'd already turned from him to examine the rock face. She had her hand pressed against one of the flat surfaces when she turned back to him to ask, "How do you think it became shaped like this?"

The sun had turned her hair to shimmering silver, her eyes to aquamarine, and seemed to bathe her features in a warm light. He was struck by the delicate lines of her small, straight nose, her softly pointed chin, her deftly curved cheeks and brow, her big, wide-set eyes, and her dainty bow-shaped mouth.

"By the hand of God," he answered, his voice oddly rough, not just thinking about the rocks.

The answer didn't seem to satisfy her. She skimmed her hand over the mostly dark gray with an occasional tinge of pink, finely grained rock surface. "It's magnificent."

Could one be jealous of stone? Clearly the stone had impressed her—which was more than he could say for himself.

He reached back through the recesses of his mind and pulled out a fact that had been buried a long time ago. "Pliny the Elder classified different kinds of rocks. He would have probably called this 'tephrias' as it appears volcanic in origin." He frowned. "Or maybe 'basanite,' which is a specific type of volcanic rock used to carve ancient statues."

She was looking at him as if he'd grown a second head. His face started to feel hot, and if he didn't know better, he would say that he was actually feeling self-conscious.

"You've read *Naturalis Historia*?" she asked, obviously shocked.

"You know Pliny?" he asked, equally so.

"A little. Unfortunately, my brothers were more interested in learning about Sparta than they were natural philosophy."

He chuckled. "I was, too, but I've always been interested in architecture." It was his passion. He could talk about it for hours. "The book on mineralogy includes information about stones for building."

IZZIE HOPED SHE DIDN'T LOOK as surprised as she felt, but she suspected her expression matched her incredulity. First the smile—the *real* smile that nearly stole her breath—and now this? *He* liked architecture? Apparently, singing wasn't the only anomaly of shared interests between them.

"I know," she said. "That's why I wished to read it as well."

She wasn't alone in her shock—or in her ability to mask it. He was just as surprised as she. "*You* are interested in architecture?"

She shrugged, a little embarrassed. Her brothers teased her about her uncommon propensity for learning by telling her that if she wasn't careful, they'd send her to a nunnery. But Randolph wasn't her family. Would he understand the curiosity that took her in strange directions of study?

"Nothing so formal," she said. "But when my brother had our donjon rebuilt—it had been hastily repaired after King Edward had it slighted in 1298—I worked with the master builder on the design. I loved it and wanted to learn more. He was the one who told me of Pliny's work—among others. I tried to interest my younger brothers with the hope that their tutor would try to procure a copy, but alas..." She shrugged.

"Sparta?" he finished with a smile that twinkled in his eyes.

She was momentarily transfixed, but then quickly managed to return his smile. But good gracious, when he smiled that way, he was so handsome, it was almost ridiculous. "Aye, I'm afraid my attempts to make rock and foundations sound as interesting to my thirteen and fourteen-year-old brothers as swords, shield walls, and ancient warriors failed miserably."

"I can't imagine why."

Izzie grinned. "Sarcasm, my lord? Have care or you will win my heart along with my cousin's, and doom me to an eternity of heartbreak."

He shook his head and held her gaze. "Somehow I don't think there is any danger of that."

A few minutes ago, she would have agreed. But she had to admit Randolph had surprised her. He was still strung too tightly and took himself far too seriously for her taste, but he did appear to have *some* sense of humor and a couple redeeming qualities beyond his good looks and charm.

She studied the handsome face looking down on her—he was at least two or three inches over six feet—with the same intensity that she'd looked at the stone earlier, trying to penetrate their secrets. To the same effect. They both revealed little.

"Perhaps you would be interested in looking at a few drawings I have of some improvements I'd like to make to my castles?"

"I would love to," Izzie said before he'd even finished.

Realizing she'd perhaps sounded a little overeager, she was trying to think of a light reply when a loud rumble shattered the peaceful quiet hum of nature around them.

She started to look around. "What was that? It sounded—"

"Watch out!" He pushed her back against the wall of rock she'd just been admiring, pinning her body to it with his own.

The shock of sensation riveted her from head to toe. She'd never been in such intimate contact with a man before and everything about it seemed to strike her at once. He was warm, solid, and very muscular. Were it not for the heat and the way her body seemed to be melting into his, she might have thought she was being pressed between *two* stone walls.

He was wearing a mail shirt but it was the solid strength of the chest underneath that she was feeling. Every ridge, every bulge, every slab, every rock-hard inch—of which there seemed to be quite a lot. Not that she was complaining. He felt good. *Really* good. Flushed cheeks and weakened knees good.

Sensing her shock—and she hoped misinterpreting it—he tried to explain what was happening before her head cleared enough to ask.

"Slide...," he started to say, but the rest of his words were drowned out by the crash of rock that rained down behind them like a deadly waterfall.

Good God! Had he not reacted as quickly as he had, she would have been crushed beneath all that. He'd saved her life—he really was a hero. The bones in her legs felt as if they'd turned to jelly. She would have slid to the ground had he not been holding her up.

Yet, through it all, he held himself like an iron cage over her. He wouldn't let anything touch her. She was perfectly safe.

She knew that. It was the only reason to explain why she didn't panic. Why she stood there calmly, concentrating on the hard warmth of his body, the steady beat of his heart, and the faint scent of rare cinnamon, while the ground reverberated and her teeth rattled with the force of the rockslide.

It lasted only a few seconds, though it felt much longer.

But when the din had faded and the dust had settled, he was still pressed against her.

The beat of his heart had been steady, but oddly she felt it pound harder now.

He turned his head enough to meet her gaze. Instinctively she sucked in her breath. There was something in his eyes she'd never seen before, but which she instinctively recognized. *Desire*. It washed over her—flooded her—with heat and awareness.

Awareness that made her heart start to pound and her body start to tingle when she felt him harden against her.

There was so much of him, it was impossible to miss. Rather than being shocked and offended, however, she became embarrassingly aroused. She flushed with heat, and a strange dampness rushed between her legs. Her body was coming alive with sensations that she couldn't seem to control.

His eyes were dark and penetrating—almost as if he were looking for something.

Permission, she realized. *He wants to kiss me.*

Her heart jumped to her throat and seemed to pound in her ears. Her eyes were telling him no... weren't they?

Apparently, they weren't inclined to lie because a second later he was lowering his mouth to hers.

Her lips parted on their own, anticipation making her forget to breathe. The air was so thick and heavy between them; her body held captive by the tight grip of desire. She couldn't have moved if she wanted to.

She didn't want to, she realized. She wanted him to kiss her. And he did. Thoroughly. Magnificently. With every bit of finesse she would have expected from someone of his reputation. Was it any surprise that Sir Thomas Randolph kissed divinely? That his lips were warm and soft and heart-wrenchingly tender? That his breath was the perfect mix of hot male and warm spice—the cinnamon she'd smelled earlier.

He was a rogue, and he kissed like one.

And from the first touch of his lips to hers, Izzie knew she was in trouble. This wasn't like any kiss she'd ever experienced. There was nothing delicate or chaste about the feel of his mouth on hers. It was searingly hot, achingly wicked, and thoroughly consuming.

The explosion of sensation shook her to the core and wouldn't let go. It penetrated in a hot wave of pleasure that radiated through her body from her head to her toes and everywhere in between, concentrating in the place between her legs where he was now wedged even more firmly.

He felt so good that she pressed herself closer. The low groan—growl?—he made in response seemed to reverberate low in her belly.

It was amazing. And then it was ever more so. The sensations grew stronger as his mouth moved over hers. Softly at first—deftly—then with increasing intensity as his tongue filled her mouth. It hit her again. His tongue was in her mouth. She'd never…

Oh God. The teasing flicks gave way to demanding strokes that seemed to reach deeper and deeper within her, making her want more. Her heart fluttered with every stroke.

She couldn't seem to get enough of his mouth and tongue as it wrapped around hers in an intimate dance. She felt greedy—insatiable—for the taste of him, for the pressure of his lips, for the pleasure he was building inside her.

For more.

He made a sound as if she might have spoken her demand aloud, and his tongue stroked deeper, harder, fiercer. Finesse and skill gave away to something else. Something even more powerful and exciting. It devoured her. *He* devoured her. Her bones seemed to dissolve as the passion enfolded them both.

His hands were still braced on either side of her head, but when she reached up to circle her arms around his neck, they slid around her to pull her fully into his embrace.

Their bodies fused together perfectly, which was why it was such a shock when he suddenly released her and stepped back with a sharp curse.

She was too busy trying to stay on her feet to notice that it was a rather crude word for such a lauded knight to utter before a lady.

But a moment later she understood what had provoked his reaction.

"Captain!" One of his men suddenly appeared around the bend in the path where Randolph and she had apparently—fortunately—been hidden from view. "We feared the worst when we heard the crash."

A second man came up beside him. "Did you not hear us calling for you?"

"I was tending to the lady," Randolph explained evenly, as if nearly ravishing someone against a wall was a daily occurrence.

Was it? She pushed the thought sharply away.

But perhaps he was more affected than he appeared—he still hadn't looked at her.

"Are you all right, my lady?" the second man asked. "Were you harmed?"

Devastated but not harmed. What had she done? How could she have let him kiss her like that? He was supposed to be courting her cousin, not kissing her. He didn't even *like* her.

"I'm fine," she assured him, pleased by the relative evenness of her own voice when her insides were a riot of emotions too tangled to analyze.

"We should get you back to the castle to make sure," Randolph said.

Their eyes met, and she felt a pinch of disappointment in her chest. The mask was firmly back in place. Whatever lightening of humor, whatever relaxing, whatever common ground they might have temporarily found had been wiped away by that kiss.

He looked just as prickly as when they'd first started out. His arrogant features were set perfectly in place. The mouth that had just plundered hers so tenderly and thoroughly was pulled in a tight line and the jaw below it had turned once again as rigid as stone.

She nodded and looked away, suddenly as eager as he to see this ride over.

CHAPTER TWO

LOST IN HER THOUGHTS IZZIE didn't notice right away that the soft buzz of conversation beside her had stopped. She was doing some needlework with some of the other women who'd joined King Robert the Bruce at Holyrood Abbey in Edinburgh. Bruce was in Edinburgh preparing for the return of the English king and his army—who were threatening to march on Scotland in the summer—by laying siege to two of the most important castles still in English hands: Edinburgh and nearby Stirling. Izzie's cousin and Elizabeth's brother, Jamie, had just captured another important castle, Roxburgh, from the English a few weeks ago.

With Edinburgh Castle under siege, the abbey was serving as a temporary court for Bruce. This afternoon, Izzie, Elizabeth, and Jamie's wife, Joanna, had joined the others in Lady Margaret Bruce's solar. The three women had set themselves off a little—Izzie wasn't alone in her unusual quiet—but it wasn't until Elizabeth spoke to her that Izzie realized Joanna had gotten up to sit with some of the women on the other side of the solar, and Izzie and her cousin were alone.

Her heart sank, anticipating what was coming. It didn't take long.

"You've been so quiet since you returned, Izzie. Did something happen on your ride today with Randolph?"

That was one way of putting it. A stab of guilt pricked her conscience. Izzie looked over at her cousin and for a moment thought about telling her the truth: *I temporarily lost my mind and let the man you are intending to marry kiss me against a cliff side… and oh yes, by the way, I might have kissed him back.*

The two cousins had always been extremely close, and Izzie suspected Elizabeth would be surprised—God knew, she certainly was—but not angry or heartbroken. It was clear this marriage, if there was to be one, was for duty and dynastic purposes, not affection. Her cousin's heart was not engaged any more than Randolph's. Nor was it likely to be, which would serve Elizabeth well when Randolph inevitably strayed from the marriage bed.

It was silly and perhaps unrealistic—fidelity was hardly common among noblemen—but Izzie wanted more from her marriage. She wasn't naive or romantic enough to think she would marry for love. Women of noble birth in her and Elizabeth's position married to forge alliances and advance their families and clans. But she wanted respect, loyalty, and affection from the man she married. Her mother had had that with her first husband, Izzie's father, but not with her second. She'd warned Izzie before she'd died not to make the same mistake—not to be fooled by a man who seemed too good to be true.

Izzie had learned the hard way that she should have listened to her. She would not make the same mistake again.

But her cousin didn't seem to have the same concerns. That she and Randolph liked one another was enough, boding well for a perfectly happy and successful noble marriage. The Douglases would benefit from Randolph's great landed wealth and royal connection, and Randolph would have Elizabeth's generous tocher and the most dazzlingly beautiful woman at court as his wife.

Her cousin was far more than that—Elizabeth was smart, accomplished, generous, and kind—but Izzie suspected the reason Randolph had been persuaded to give up his prized bachelorhood was because he knew he would be unlikely to find a more "perfect" bride to complement his "perfect" knight. With her blond hair, big blue eyes, and poppet-like features, Elizabeth looked like a faerie princess drawn straight from the pages of a children's tale, and not surprisingly Randolph had claimed the part of the handsome prince by her side. The abbey was already buzzing with admiration for the two after Randolph's grandiose "romantic" greeting the other night, riding into the abbey yard in full, shiny mail on a great black charger and dropping to his knee to kiss Elizabeth's hand.

How could Izzie compete with a faerie tale?

Not that she wanted to, although she had to admit she'd had a few—maybe more than a few—confused thoughts after that kiss. Something tugged in her chest, perilously close to her heart. For a moment…

For a moment she'd been half-crazed. She must have been to have succumbed so easily to that kiss and the man who'd wielded it so expertly—Lord knew, he must have had enough practice. "What's not to love?" Well, it certainly wasn't the way he kissed. Sir Too-Good-To-Be-True was indeed too good to be true in that regard.

Had she actually thought even for a minute that she'd felt something special? What she'd felt was desire.

The physical reaction was hardly unexpected. He is gorgeous, who wouldn't be attracted to him?

Your cousin for one, a little voice pointed out. It was true; if Elizabeth was attracted to him, she hid it well.

But Izzie pushed that annoying voice aside. Just because *she* was attracted to him, didn't mean anything. She wasn't going to let one kiss make her act like a silly, starry-eyed maid with dreams of fate and everlasting love.

Not with Sir Thomas Randolph, at least. He wasn't for her any more than she was for him. Izzie wasn't beautiful and accomplished like her cousin. She was more want-to-be scholar than princess or suitable consort for a hero, content to stay in the background rather than be the center of attention. Randolph and her cousin were the same in that regard, both seemed to have been made to be on pedestals and to shine. Although Izzie had been told she was pretty, she was a mere mortal and not in her cousin's realm of jaw-dropping beauty. Izzie was even-tempered and made people laugh with her wry—sometimes mischievous—observations, but she certainly didn't dazzle.

Why Randolph had kissed her, Izzie didn't know. But she wasn't going to let it upset her cousin's plans. If she told Elizabeth about the kiss, Izzie had no doubt her cousin would read something more into it than there was and insist on stepping aside—even if there was nothing to step aside for.

Nay, Izzie thought. If this betrothal didn't happen, it wasn't going to be because of her.

She wondered if it might be about someone else though. Not wanting to lie to her cousin, she decided to turn the question back to her. "I was going to say the same about you," she said. "Where were you going earlier that you forgot about your ride with Randolph?" Elizabeth opened her mouth to respond, but Izzie stopped her. "And don't tell me it was an errand for Joanna—unless that errand had something to do with Thom MacGowan."

Elizabeth's mouth snapped closed. Apparently, she had no more wish to talk about the earlier events in the day than Izzie. It took Elizabeth some time to reply. "I did go see Thom, but it was an errand for Jo. Truly."

She looked so distressed that Izzie forgot all about Randolph and reached out to comfort her cousin, putting her hand on her arm. "Did something happen, Ella?" she asked, using her cousin's childhood nickname.

"Yes. No. I mean…" Elizabeth put down the piece of embroidery she was working on—a banner for her brother Jamie—and her hands started to twist anxiously in her lap. "I don't know."

Izzie didn't press. It was clear Elizabeth *didn't* know, and this was something she'd have to figure out herself.

Izzie didn't envy her. It was obvious her cousin had strong feelings for Thom MacGowan, but he was too far beneath her in rank to even be considered a suitor. The son of the village blacksmith might be a soldier now, but Elizabeth was the sister of one of Bruce's most important lieutenants. Indeed, James had risen high enough to arrange an alliance between his sister and the king's nephew, Randolph—the other of the king's most important lieutenants and Jamie's usually friendly rival.

For the past couple of years, Jamie and Randolph had been engaged in what seemed like a back-and-forth contest of extraordinary feats of war to win the position of the king's right-hand man. Izzie thought it was rather silly—the king had two hands, why couldn't they each have one?—but she had to admit, it was exciting to watch them try to outdo one another. With Jamie's recent achievement in taking Roxburgh Castle (in dramatic fashion of course), Randolph was probably chomping at the bit to do something more extraordinary in taking Edinburgh. A siege hardly qualified, which undoubtedly frustrated him to no end. It wouldn't make for a very good story.

Their short conversation had visibly distressed her cousin, and not long after Joanna rejoined them, Elizabeth made excuses to return to her solar.

"Izzie and I won't be much longer," Joanna let her know. "It will be time to ready for the evening meal soon."

"I think I'll just stay in my room tonight," Elizabeth said. "I'm tired. I'm going to read a book and try to retire early."

Izzie quirked a brow at that. Thom MacGowan must *really* have her cousin confused for Elizabeth to be reduced to picking up a book. Her cousin had never enjoyed learning as Izzie had. *"Not all of us are born to be clerks."* Randolph was right about that.

Nonetheless, skipping the evening meal sounded like a good idea—avoiding Randolph might have occurred to her—and Izzie was tempted to do the same, but her stomach was loudly reminding her that she hadn't eaten since morning. The planned midday feast in a basket she and Randolph were supposed to enjoy on their ride had been forgotten after the rockslide and disastrous kiss that followed. But she was remembering it now. The meal, not the kiss. The kiss she had forgotten.

Liar.

Well, even if she hadn't quite forgotten it, she'd put it in perspective. Sir Thomas Randolph was a handsome rogue, who could kiss like the Devil, but like a sugary confection, he would satisfy in the moment and only leave her wanting. She wanted genuine substance, not superficial charms. In other words, she didn't want a faerie tale; she wanted something *real*.

Besides, she thought with a laugh. When was the last time the hero of the story rode off with the decidedly nondazzling, scholarly cousin? No one would want to read that story—people liked extraordinary.

But Izzie forgot that she'd always had a sweet tooth.

BY THE TIME IZZIE WALKED into the rectory for the evening meal, she *had* forgotten that kiss.

But it took just one look over at the dais for all the feelings, all the confusion, all the desire to come rushing back. The memories hit her hard, leaving all that wonderful perspective she'd developed decidedly cracked.

Perhaps she needed a bit more time? She wasn't *that* hungry. A low rumble from her stomach belied that claim. Still, recognizing when a retreat was in order, she would have turned right around if her cousin Jamie and his wife, Joanna, hadn't come up behind her.

"All alone, Izzie?" Jamie asked. "Where's my sister?"

It was sometimes hard to believe that her cousin Jamie had become one of the most feared men in England. But the dark frown on his face reminded her why the English called him "the Black" Douglas.

It was clear he was suspicious of something. Probably exactly what Izzie was suspicious of—that something was going on between his sister and Thom MacGowan. From what Izzie could tell, Thom and Jamie didn't like one another, though supposedly they had once been the best of friends.

Izzie caught Joanna's gaze, but the gentle pleading there

wasn't necessary. She wasn't going to get between the two siblings on this one—she'd learned her lesson a long time ago not to try to mediate Jamie and Elizabeth's many battles.

"She wasn't hungry and said she was going to read a book and try to get to bed early," Izzie said.

Jamie's frown only deepened, and Izzie realized her mistake. She'd thought the same thing when Elizabeth had made the excuse.

"Ella, stay in her room to read and avoid a meal and entertainment? That sounds more like you, Izzie. We always had to pull your nose out of a book to do anything." He tweaked that nose fondly. "Maybe I should have Helen MacKay check in on her." Helen was a gifted healer. "Ella has a big week ahead of her, I do not want her to be fighting sickness."

Izzie felt a strange twist in her stomach, realizing to what he referred: the betrothal that seemed all but preordained. Though Randolph and Jamie were known for their fierce rivalry, Izzie knew that Jamie was just as eager for this engagement as Elizabeth—perhaps more so. Allying himself with the king's nephew would be a gold spur on her ambitious cousin's boot.

"She's fine, Jamie," Izzie assured him. "Just tired, that's all."

Suddenly, he seemed to remember something and smiled. "Ah, that's right. She was to go riding with Randolph today, wasn't she?" He chuckled. "I'll have to have a word with him about tiring her out."

Izzie tried to hide her alarm, but Joanna wasn't quite as successful. Her eyes widened. Clearly she didn't want her husband to learn about his sister's change of plans. Joanna had made no secret of her hope that Elizabeth would choose Thom MacGowan over Randolph.

"You promised you'd stay out of it, James," Joanna admonished. "If this betrothal is meant to be, it will happen without your forcing it." Before he could argue, which he looked about to, Joanna shifted his attention back to the room. "Come, I'm hungry, and the king is calling for you."

Realizing that there was no turning back now, Izzie squared her shoulders and marched forward behind them. She would have to face Randolph at some point; she might as well get it over with.

Really, she was making too much of this. They'd shared a kiss—so what? She certainly wasn't going to start writing his name in the margins of her portfolios or on the pages of her precious parchment. The thought made her smile. Lady Isabel Randolph, Countess of Moray… *that* would be about as likely as snow falling in hell or Randolph declaring his love for her—and her believing him.

Now she was laughing. Which turned out to be the perfect or perfectly wrong thing, depending on how you looked at it, as it was at that moment that their eyes met.

She'd done it again. Once again he'd assumed he was the reason for her amusement—which in this case he admittedly was—and his expression grew as dark as a thundercloud.

She quickly sobered and looked around for a seat on the far side of the dais—preferably as far away from Randolph as she could get. Unfortunately, the benches were all full. The king motioned Jamie and Joanna to sit by him, and all that was left was a small space beside Randolph that he had probably been saving for Elizabeth.

With a sigh of inevitability—why wouldn't the only available seat be next to him?—Izzie waited for him to stand (which with atypical *un*gallantry took him a few seconds too long) and slid in beside him on the bench. It was a tight squeeze, and she was embarrassingly conscious of the strong, abundantly muscled body pressed against hers. Again. *Don't think of that.*

"I'm afraid my cousin is not joining us tonight," she explained with a twist of her mouth that told him she had guessed his thoughts. "She decided to retire early." Her smile deepened. "I would have done the same, but it turns out I'm quite hungry after missing the midday meal."

She'd only meant it as a gentle teasing—a way to hopefully prevent any awkwardness over what had happened earlier—but he, of course, seemed to take it the wrong way. He looked either horrified or as if he'd just eaten a bad piece of beef, she couldn't decide which. In any event, apparently, she'd brought up a subject that wasn't supposed to be mentioned or alluded to at all. Well, if he wanted to pretend it never happened, that was fine by her.

She felt his impressive shoulders stiffen, which was unfortunate, as it reminded her of how wonderful all those muscles had felt wrapped around her, and made her want to do something silly like put her hands on either side of his neck and knead all the tension from those taut shoulders and arms.

"I apologize," he started stiffly.

But she cut him off. "No apologies are necessary, my lord. I meant nothing by it. Truly, it was not a criticism, a reprimand, or a reminder—just a poor attempt to make a jest." Her mouth quirked. "I forgot that you do not find my jests amusing."

She was rewarded by an easing of the tension in his shoulders and the barest hint of a smile hovering around the edge of his mouth.

Mouth. Not the thing to think about. If she did, she would remember...

Her body flushed with heat and she quickly averted her gaze away from the wicked and embarrassingly visceral memories.

"I do believe they are beginning to grow on me," he said dryly.

"Like the plague?"

"Nay, nothing so deadly. I was thinking more in line of a wart or a mole."

She laughed. Dear lord, this was becoming a regular occurrence. Pretty soon, she would have to admit that he actually was amusing. At least when he was like this, dry, blunt, and honest. She doubted there were many women he would say such a thing to.

"Such flattery, my lord. You do know how to charm a lady. I've always dreamed of being compared to a wart."

"Or a mole."

She laughed again. "Of course, how could I leave that out? Perhaps one day you might compose a chanson about it?"

"Tempt me enough, and I just might."

"Why does it seem as if a gauntlet has just been thrown down?" She smiled mischievously. "How shall I tempt you?"

It took her a moment to realize what she'd said—and how it might be interpreted. That's not what she meant. She meant tempt him by annoying him, which is what she seemed to have a talent for doing. But it could also have been meant flirtatiously.

She wasn't flirtatious. And she wanted to tell him so, but if the flare of heat in his gaze was any indication, it was too late for that.

And just like that, the awkwardness and the tension returned full force. But it was a different kind of tension. It was the tension between two people who'd shared intimacy—passion—and were both remembering it.

CHAPTER THREE

AS RANDOLPH COULDN'T VERY WELL tell her just how tempting he found her, he let the conversation drop. Fortunately, his Aunt Margaret Bruce (the youngest of Bruce's sisters who was actually ten years younger than Randolph's nine and twenty—his mother had been considerably older than her half-siblings) was seated on his left, and he spent most of the meal listening to her impressions of Edinburgh, which she was visiting for the first time.

At the outset of the war, the king's two youngest sisters, Margaret and Matilda, had been sent to Bergen, Norway, where their eldest sister had been queen. The two girls had returned to Scotland a couple of years ago, but had remained in the north at Kildrummy Castle until recently.

As entertaining as his young aunt might be, however, Randolph spent most of the meal trying to pretend he wasn't aware of every movement, every breath, every word coming out of the sinfully delicious mouth of the woman pressed up against his right side. Who would have thought that someone who could irritate him so profusely would taste so sweet?

Maybe if he hadn't had that same softly curved body pressed up against his earlier in an even more intimate fashion, he wouldn't be so conscious of how good she felt. He wouldn't be so hot. And he wouldn't remember how he'd hardened against her like a lad.

Christ. Just thinking about it made his face flush. To a

man of his experience it was bloody humiliating.

But he hadn't felt lust like that in a while. Hell, he couldn't remember *ever* feeling lust like that—although he was sure that he must have at some point. He frowned. Of course, he must have.

Still, the lack of control had been a surprise. As had been that kiss. How had it spun out of control so quickly? One minute he'd been thinking that he had to taste her, and the next he'd been thinking about wrapping her legs around his hips and swiving her senseless.

She'd been so warm and soft and surprisingly sweet, he'd found himself drowning. Melting. Losing all sense of time and place and right and wrong. He was about to ask her cousin to marry him, for Devil's sake! What had he been thinking?

He knew exactly what he'd been thinking. He'd been thinking how good she felt, and how he wanted to feel all that soft warmth surrounding him.

But it was her passionate response that undid him. *That* he hadn't anticipated. Although perhaps he should have. A woman who laughed so freely and with such ease would know how to find pleasure in life.

Find pleasure. He nearly groaned. An image of her lying in his bed—naked—with her hand stroking between her legs while he watched made him hard all over again.

Bloody hell, he shouldn't be thinking things like that. Not when they were seated practically on top of one another. He shifted in his seat, but it didn't do any good. They were still touching, and his cock was still rock hard and throbbing uncomfortably in his suddenly too-tight braies.

Damn these benches to hell! It seemed like half the nobles in the city were crammed around the long trestle table on the dais. There was one man in particular he wouldn't mind knocking off, although until about a half hour ago, he'd considered Sir Gilbert de la Haye a good friend.

Lady Isabel laughed for what must have been the fifth or

sixth time—not that he was counting, blast it!—and Randolph felt the muscles at the back of his neck bunch. What the Devil was de la Haye saying to her? Randolph had never known him to be so bloody amusing. The respected knight in the king's retinue was about as stoic and serious as they came. But Lady Isabel seemed to find him hilarious.

Randolph gritted his teeth, but he couldn't help listening. She had the most entrancing laugh. It was soft and soothing, like the gentle tinkle of water over rocks in a slow running burn. And there was something oddly contagious about it—something that made him want to laugh, too, despite his irritation.

Why the hell was he so irritated anyway? He should be glad she was trying to make the best of a decidedly awkward situation by shamelessly flirting with de la Haye. It was so obvious that she was trying to make him jealous. Randolph knew she could not be as immune to him as she was pretending—he'd seen that blush earlier.

Although she certainly wasn't acting like she was aware of him at all right now. But that's what it had to be—an act. She couldn't be pressed up against him and not be thinking about that kiss. Not when he—who had far more experiences in these things—could think of nothing else.

She leaned over to listen to something de la Haye was saying in a low voice. The sly bastard had done it on purpose! The movement caused her bodice to shift, revealing at least another half inch of the perfect swell of her breasts. Randolph went rigid with rage when de la Haye glanced down into that deep cleft... Bloody hell, the blackguard! Randolph's fist might have ended up through the other man's teeth rather than squeezing around his goblet until his knuckles turned white if his aunt hadn't said something.

"Is something wrong, nephew?" his aunt Margaret asked with a smile—she loved teasing him about her supposed position of seniority despite their differences in age. "I asked how the siege was going, but I guess you didn't hear me?" She glanced at Lady Isabel with a little too much understanding.

The glance acted like a hard shake of sanity. What the hell was he doing? He'd given his word to Douglas that he would ask for his sister. He wouldn't go back on that. He'd worked too hard to put past mistakes behind him and was careful about everything he did—extremely careful. Besides, Elizabeth Douglas was perfect for him and exactly what he wanted in a wife. She wasn't just rich, beautiful, and well connected—all of which were important—she loved the excitement of court life as much as he did. She was well versed in many subjects, understood the politics of court, and would be an asset to his plans. He shouldn't be dallying with her cousin. Admittedly, it wasn't the first time he'd found himself in an unexpected passionate embrace with a woman, but he sure as hell didn't go around ravishing virgins. Until today, that is.

He had to put a stop to this. If his aunt was noticing something between them, anyone could. At the first opportunity, he would talk to Lady Isabel and apologize. As young and inexperienced as she was, she was probably confused, and he didn't want her to get the wrong idea about what had happened.

For now, however, he turned his full attention to his aunt, answering her questions about the siege, which frankly wasn't progressing at all. The English didn't seem inclined to surrender any time soon, and Randolph knew that if the Scots were going to take the castle before Edward of England marched next summer, they'd have to think of something inventive. He wasn't going to let Douglas get the better of him, damn it.

When he'd heard about Thom MacGowan's climbing skills in rescuing Douglas's brother, Randolph had gone to his uncle with an idea about putting those skills to use in Edinburgh. But apparently Castle Rock, as the cliff upon which Edinburgh Castle sat was known, was even too dangerous for MacGowan's extraordinary climbing skills. But Randolph wasn't giving up completely on the idea of finding a route up through the cliff. It was too tantalizing a prospect. Climbing a cliff no one had ever climbed before to take a castle? It would make him a legend.

The evening meal wasn't the prolonged affair of the usual midday meal, and given the Lenten season and that they were in an abbey, it was also fairly subdued. It wasn't long before the king stood, signaling the unofficial end to the meal, and the others began to follow.

As soon as Randolph heard Lady Isabel start to thank de la Haye for "such an enjoyable meal," he was ready.

"A moment, my lady. If you don't mind, there is something I would like to talk to you about before you retire."

She frowned. If he wasn't so certain that her indifference was an act, he might think that his request was an imposition.

"I'm quite tired, my lord. Do you mind if we wait until tomorrow? Sir Gilbert has offered to escort me to the guesthouse."

It certainly sounded as if it were an imposition as well. It was his turn to frown. "I am happy to escort you. I'm sure Sir Gilbert won't mind."

He gave his longtime companion-in-arms a look of warning, which the other man heeded with a speculative lift of his brow. "Not at all," de la Haye said gamely. He wasn't a fool. He wouldn't challenge a warrior of Randolph's skill. But de la Haye also wouldn't back down completely, and added provocatively to Isabel, "As long as you promise I may do so another night this week."

If he was trying to anger Randolph—which he probably was—it worked. Randolph's eyes narrowed, and the other man smiled as if he'd just made an interesting discovery. Whatever de la Haye thought he knew, he was wrong. Randolph wasn't jealous. He didn't get jealous. It was a wasted emotion—as so many emotions were. He liked women, they liked him. Why did it need to be any more complicated than that? Keep it simple. He'd seen too many of his friends act like idiots over women. But he was fortunate to be immune to those kinds of feelings. And he had no intention of letting that change. His focus was on one thing and one thing only: winning the war and cementing his position as Robert the Bruce's greatest knight.

Douglas might disagree with that title—especially after his dramatic taking of Roxburgh Castle—but Randolph had no doubt that he would come out on top. If he could just figure out a way to take the damn castle. Preferably by something dramatic. He needed a little excitement. More than two months of sieging was wearing on him.

"Of course," Lady Isabel said, looking back and forth between the two men as if understanding that something was going on, but not sure what. Finally, her gaze rested on de la Haye. "Whenever you can tear yourself away from the siege again. Besides you did promise to show me those drawings."

Randolph didn't like the sound of that. "What drawings?"

Lady Isabel smiled conspiratorially at de la Haye before turning to Randolph. The smile fell from her face. "Nothing that would interest you, my lord." She stood. "If you are ready?" Without waiting for him, she gave de la Haye a nod and started off.

Randolph had to hurry to catch up to her, which he did just as she exited the refectory and started down the steps to the yard.

She was bloody wrong. He was *very* interested. Didn't she know drawings were a euphemism men used to lure unsuspecting innocents to their chambers?

He put his hand on her arm, turned her toward him, and told her so—along with an admonishment to stay away from de la Haye.

She looked at him as if he were crazed—which wasn't that far from how he was feeling—and burst out laughing. He sensed a few eyes on them as more people flooded out of the refectory and dispersed across the yard. "Are you serious?" She laughed some more. "I can assure you Sir Gilbert has no nefarious purpose in mind. He is a kind and honorable man."

De la Haye was a fierce and ruthless warrior who has had an eye for pretty ladies since the death of his wife a few years back. Feeling conspicuous standing there in the middle of the yard, and aware that they were attracting attention, Randolph pulled her into a small walled garden. "And you've made this determination after knowing him what, an hour?"

She shrugged and crossed her arms. "Some men are easy to figure out."

Now why did he feel as if that were directed at someone other than de la Haye?

With a deep sigh, as if the conversation was wearying her and she just wanted it done, she added, "I hardly think he was trying to lure me with drawings done by his five-year-old daughter that featured the last nursemaid he'd hired to look after her, whom she'd turned into a dragon, and then a gorgon. Apparently, the child is having some difficulty after losing her mother and thinks that any woman in the household is a threat. But the drawings were very good, and he wondered if I might know someone who could encourage her to use her talents in a more productive way."

Pop. Just like that the bubble of anger and indignation burst, leaving him feeling rather silly. Perhaps he'd overreacted just a little. "Oh."

She gave him an amused look as if reading his thoughts. "As I recall you asked me to look at some drawings as well?"

Damn, she was right. She laughed at his chagrined expression. "Besides, I think you are hardly in any position to be casting stones, my lord."

He stiffened at the jab that was not unwarranted. "That is what I should like to talk to you about."

IZZIE REGRETTED BRINGING THE SUBJECT up. That was the last thing she wanted to talk about. She was doing her best to forget it ever happened, but he wasn't making it easy.

Just sitting next to him at the meal had brought back all sorts of unwanted memories.

"There is no need, my lord," she protested, wrapping her cloak around her shoulders. The wind had picked up a little and although they were protected in the monk's herb garden—she could smell the rosemary and thyme with each gust—it was still a cool evening.

Randolph wasn't inclined to listen to her wishes. He was a man on a mission and would not be turned from his course. "Yes, there is. I owe you an apology."

Izzie squirmed a little. Dear Lord this was awkward. Did they really need to talk about this? "You don't owe me—"

"I make no excuse. I don't know what came over me, but I apologize and can assure you it will never happen again."

He stood there so stiffly and awkwardly, something about the situation was so ridiculous, she couldn't resist saying, "If you don't know what came over you, how can you be sure it won't happen again?"

He seemed taken aback by the question and didn't realize that she hadn't meant it seriously. "Because it can't... for obvious reasons."

"Because you intend to marry my cousin?"

"Aye, among other reasons. Surely you can see..." He seemed unusually lost for words. "You... me... It isn't possible."

Surely. It was obvious. As there could be no objection to her family or tocher—she was nearly her cousin's equal in both—there was only one thing left: her. Obviously she wasn't dazzling enough for him, and the wife of a great hero had to dazzle.

Suddenly, she didn't feel like jesting anymore; she just wanted the conversation over. "Of course." She took a few steps toward the yard. "Now, if you'll excuse me."

"Wait," he said, stopping her by taking her arm. "I don't mean to upset you. I just didn't want you to be confused or jump to any conclusions."

She turned around slowly, her tone deceptively even. "What kind of conclusions might those be?"

Clearly, he wasn't prepared for her question as it had him flustered. "You are young and innocent. I was trying to have care for your tender feelings."

She stared at him incredulously, trying not to laugh, but his arrogance was truly too much to be borne. "My what?"

"It was just a kiss. I know the feelings can be overwhelming and confusing to young ladies and..." He shrugged uncomfortably. "I just don't want you to read too much into it."

She couldn't hold it back this time; she laughed in his face. After one kiss—admittedly a spectacular one—the arrogant swine thought she was half in love with him!

"You need not worry on my account, Sir Thomas." She dismissed his concerns with a smile. "I'm not likely to read too much into something so little. What happened earlier was nothing more than a reaction to the danger of the situation. It might have happened with anyone."

"Little?" he growled angrily, clearly not appreciating her cavalier take on things. He'd put himself in the role of the one to do the letting down easily and didn't like that she wasn't playing her part. "I don't know how many times you've been kissed, my lady, but nothing about that kiss was little."

She lifted a brow, lazily, though inside she could feel anger begin to overtake amusement. Did he have any idea how offensive he was being? How he'd just assumed someone like her—someone so obviously out of his realm of spectacular—would be unable to resist his vaunted charms?

Someone needed to knock the arrogant prig down a peg or two. Why shouldn't she have the pleasure? "Enough times to know the difference between meaningful and meaningless—or to not confuse sentiment with lust." The hand holding her arm tightened and his expression turned so fierce she almost reconsidered. But he needed to hear this. "I know this might come as a shock to you, my lord, but not every woman whom you kiss is going to fall in love with you—especially me. When I fall in love, it will be with someone who knows how to laugh at himself, who doesn't mind making a few mistakes, who doesn't think the world is his personal stage, and who has something meaningful to say beyond what he thinks I want to hear. I want someone who values loyalty"—he seemed to flinch, but it didn't stop her—"and fidelity, not someone who thinks his manhood lies beneath his belt. But most of all I want someone who is capable of feeling—true feeling—and that, my lord, is not you."

His face had gone white with anger, which, it turned out, was actually more intimidating than dark. He looked as though he couldn't decide whether to shake her or pull her into his arms and kiss her.

She blanched. Knowing she couldn't let that happen— the kiss, not the shake, not if she wanted her words to mean anything—she jerked away. "I think we've both said more than enough on the subject. If you will excuse me, I will bid you good night."

She didn't give him a chance to respond. She turned and fled into the safety of the darkness, where he wouldn't be able to see the glistening of tears that she couldn't explain— even to herself.

CHAPTER FOUR

DAWN CAME TOO QUICKLY. IT seemed as if Izzie had just fallen asleep when the first piercing rays of sunlight poked through the cracks of the shutters in the small third-floor chamber that she shared with her cousin.

She rolled onto her back and heaved a heavy sigh. She hadn't had enough sleep to make everything that had happened the evening before seem inconsequential on reflection. She was still embarrassed by her outburst and by her reaction. Despite the fact that she'd meant every word she'd said, somehow Randolph with his assumptions and arrogance had slipped under her defenses. As much as she didn't want to admit it, he'd hurt her. It was one thing to know they would never suit and another to have it pointed out—by assuming it was obvious.

At least neither of them would be suffering under any illusions now. After what she'd said, he would probably be just as eager to avoid her as she was him.

Careful not to wake her cousin and the maidservant who slept in the mural chamber, Izzie donned her oldest, plainest gown—one of the Cistercian nuns at the hospital would have an old apron she could borrow to put over it—ran a comb through her hair before weaving it in a plait, washed her face, rubbed her teeth with a cloth before rinsing her mouth with her favorite mint and wine mixture, and tiptoed out of the room.

With what she'd offered to help the nuns with at the hospital today, she hardly needed to look her best. She smiled, thinking that the day's hard labor in the garden would be a good way to keep her mind off of... everything.

Although it was a short walk from the abbey up the high street to the hospital, she found one of her cousin Jamie's men to escort her. When she'd first gone to stay with her Douglas kin at Blackhouse Tower, she wouldn't have dreamed of leaving without a handful of men to protect her. But with the passing three months, having heard nothing from Sir Stephen, she'd gradually relaxed her guard and come to the realization that she had overreacted.

The threat she'd sensed that had caused her to flee halfway across Scotland to seek refuge with her powerful cousin—what man in his right mind would challenge the Black Douglas?—had never materialized. Sir Stephen Dunbar hadn't been waiting behind the next tree or shadowy corridor to what...? Capture her? It seemed so silly now. As if she'd heard too many tales of abducted brides.

But it hadn't seemed so silly then. Then she'd been terrified of the dashing young knight who at first had swept her off her feet—literally, she recalled, thinking of how he'd insisted on carrying her over every muddy patch of grass on that day they'd walked to the coast—but who had turned into an ogre when she'd learned the truth and refused his offer of marriage.

When Sir Stephen, who'd fostered with her eldest brother, Alexander, arrived at Bonkyll Castle under the pretense of needing to speak to him, she'd been surprised. He should know that Alexander had been away for months fighting for Bruce under their kinsman and her guardian, Walter Stewart, and wasn't expected home for a few weeks. She'd believed Sir Stephen when he said he must have misunderstood her brother's intentions.

She'd believed him because she wanted to believe him. Because he was handsome and charming and looked at her with a dazed look in his eyes as if he'd been struck by cupid's arrow the moment he'd seen her. He'd spent two weeks wooing her, making her laugh, and making her feel as if she was the most special woman in the world.

She was half in love with him by the time he asked her to marry him. She would have accepted, and probably would have run off with him to be married without her cousin Walter's permission—he held her marriage rights—if her brother hadn't arrived home early and told her the truth. Sir Stephen had borrowed a great deal of money from him and was having trouble repaying the debt. She—and her tocher—were to be the answer to his troubles.

If he seems too good to be true, he probably is. Too late, she recalled her mother's warning.

She shivered, remembering Sir Stephen's cold rage when she'd informed him of her decision. There was something hard and calculating in his eyes that had made her think he wasn't going to accept her refusal. Her brother, too, had been worried enough by what had happened to send her to Jamie and Elizabeth "until things settled down."

In other words, until he and Walter could find her a husband. Only marriage would truly protect her from a man of Sir Stephen's ilk. It was time. As much as she liked her independence, she could not put it off any longer.

Izzie knew she had been luckier than most to have remained unwed for this long. Women in her position were often promised at a very young age, and certainly betrothed before the "advanced" age of two and twenty. If her father had lived, no doubt she would have been. There had been a few discussions since her mother's death, but Walter—young himself—had never pressed her.

But after he'd learned about Sir Stephen's treachery, the frequency of the topic between them had increased. It seemed to be the first thing he said to her after greeting her. "Hullo, cousin. Any contenders yet?"

She might have been picking a prized bull at market.

The thought made her smile as she entered the hospital. The prioress wasn't ready for her yet, so Izzie decided to look in on Annie, the very sick young girl who'd been so charmed by Randolph the other day.

Upon entering the second-floor chamber where the most seriously ill patients were housed, Izzie glanced down the line of pallets that seemed to cover every inch of floor space to the one by the window. Her heart stopped. Seeing the empty pallet, she feared the worst. It was Annie's pallet. She liked to watch the birds who'd made a nest under the roof, and the other occupants—all much older—had insisted the young girl take the prime location.

The older woman on the pallet beside Annie's must have guessed her thoughts. "The wee one is fine," she said. "She has a visitor who took her outside in the garden."

Relief turned quickly to alarm—it was a cool morning. "In her condition? She'll catch a chill."

"I don't think so," the old woman chortled.

But Izzie wasn't listening. She was already halfway down the stairs. What visitor? To her knowledge Annie was an orphan who had been left at the hospital by relatives who could no longer care for her. Izzie hastened across the hall, through the kitchens, and then outside into the—

Garden. She stopped in her tracks and blinked, her brain refusing to believe the sight beheld by her eyes.

My God. The rush of emotion at the scene before her was surprisingly strong, bringing an odd tightness to her chest and heat to her throat. It was a little hard to breathe, and her heart was beating funny.

A man knelt beside a stone bench that had been stacked high with pillows—probably most of the feather pillows in the hospital—and cradled in the middle of that fluffy makeshift bed, bundled from head to toe in blankets, was a tiny figure. Annie. The man was pointing to something in the small pond, which the girl had obviously been positioned to enjoy.

Although the man had his back to Izzie, and he was dressed in simple soldier's garb of black leather breaches and a matching *cotum,* she recognized him instantly. Randolph. Here. Alone. Without his retinue or crowd of admiring spectators, to visit a little girl whom most noblemen wouldn't notice, let alone take time to see. She couldn't believe it.

I've misjudged him. The truth hit her hard. It wasn't all

an act; not everything was about appearances and image. He wasn't without feelings at all. For the first time she felt like she was seeing the real man. A man who was being kind for kindness's sake, not because of how it would look. There was no one here to see him, and by the looks of his understated attire—not a glint of shining mail or colorful, emblazoned with arms tabard in sight—he was trying not to attract attention. But to her, he'd never looked more heroic. Maybe he wasn't too good to be true. Maybe he was just… good.

Izzie drew a little closer, curious to hear what they were talking about.

"I wish that I could see it," Annie said. "I'm sure there will be a great celebration when you take the castle from the English, my lord."

Izzie realized Randolph hadn't been pointing to the pond but to the castle poised on the giant black rock that hovered over the city of Edinburgh like a sentinel. The church was higher on the hill that separated the abbey from the castle, and the view from this prospect was even more dramatic.

"And you shall," Randolph said, something catching in his voice. Izzie felt the same thing happening in her chest, suspiciously near her heart. They both knew how unlikely it would be for the girl to outlive the siege. "I will see to it myself."

Annie gazed up at him; a soulful, too-wise expression on the face of one so young. "Thank you for sending your healer, my lord. But I know Lady Helen told you there was nothing that could be done."

Randolph didn't say anything, but the sadness and pity in his expression said it all.

He'd brought Lady Helen to see the girl? Izzie had traveled with the vaunted healer and her husband Magnus MacKay from Roxburgh to Edinburgh. Why hadn't she thought of it herself? She felt as though she was seeing him through different eyes. She was still attracted to him, but that attraction went far deeper than his too-handsome face.

"You are very kind," Annie said. "But you do not need

to worry. I am going to a better place."

Izzie felt her heart tug again, hearing what the young girl hadn't said. The life of an impoverished orphan was a difficult one. Most of what she'd known must have been misery and hardship. Heaven would seem an escape from hunger, squalor, and illness that had dominated her earthly life.

Randolph seemed to understand as well. He squeezed Annie's hand. "You are indeed."

"There was another girl about my age here not long ago. She said that in heaven she would be a princess." She looked up at Randolph with hope shimmering in her eyes. "Do you think that is true, my lord?"

Randolph's voice was perilously low and thick as if he were fighting the same feelings burning Izzie's throat and eyes. It was emotion, she realized. *Genuine* emotion. He wasn't incapable after all. "I'm certain of it."

"What do you think, my lady?" Annie asked, glancing over her shoulder at Izzie with a wan smile, the effort alone an exertion.

Both Izzie and Randolph started—Izzie for not realizing she'd been seen, and Randolph for not realizing she was there. Randolph immediately jumped to his feet.

Izzie walked toward them. "I am certain of it as well. Besides, Sir Thomas would know. He's an earl, and the nephew of the king, which is almost like a prince."

Laughter lit Annie's face and for a moment Isabel could see the girl she might have been had life not treated her so cruelly. "Does that mean you shall be a princess when you and Sir Thomas wed, my lady?" Annie mistook the sudden shocked silence that had suddenly filled the garden and explained, "I overheard some of the nuns after you left last time. They said Sir Thomas was to marry one of the ladies, and I knew it had to be you."

Izzie hoped her expression didn't show her horror and embarrassment. How could Annie think she and Randolph…? No one who saw them would put them together, especially with her gorgeous cousin around. So why then was she suddenly eager to ask her why she'd thought that?

She glanced at Randolph who seemed to have recovered faster than she. He gave a slight shake of his head, which Izzie understood: don't make her feel badly.

Izzie forced a smile to her face. "Aye, I suppose I shall— or as close to one as anyone could ever dream to be." Anyone such as her cousin. Eager to switch the subject, Izzie added, "How long have you been out here?"

"Not very long," Annie answered quickly.

Randolph gave the young girl a pointed look with an arched brow. "About a quarter of an hour longer than you talked me into. I said a half hour. You shouldn't be out here much longer than that."

Annie started to protest. "But I'm plenty warm—"

Randolph stopped her by sweeping her up in his arms. "No arguing, little one. You don't want to see the lady become angry with me, do you?" He leaned down to say in a low voice that Izzie could still hear. "She's quite fierce when she's angry, you know."

Annie glanced over his shoulder to Izzie, looking skeptical. "I can't imagine the lady would ever be angry with you, Sir Thomas. You are the most wonderful knight in the kingdom."

Randolph grinned and looked right at Izzie, daring her to argue. "Did you hear that, Lady Isabel?"

Izzie sighed and shook her head. "I heard it."

He grinned, and she felt the force of that roguish, I-dare-you-not-to-fall-in-love-with-me smile hit her like a fist in her chest.

Realizing that she didn't want to take that dare, she followed the famous knight carrying the bundled up young peasant girl back into the building.

RANDOLPH SENSED LADY ISABEL WATCHING him, but she didn't say anything until they were leaving the room.

"You gave her your cloak, didn't you? I saw her try to hand it back to you."

He shrugged. "I have others. She needs it more than me. The fur will keep her warm."

"It must have cost a fortune."

He didn't say anything. It had, but he could afford another.

"I'm sure she will treasure it for…" Her voice dropped off.

For as long as she lives.

They walked down the stairs together in silence. There was no need to say anything. What *could* they say? It was sad, horrible, wrong, and far too common an occurrence. Randolph had been visiting poor houses and hospitals since he was a child. His mother had insisted that he be raised to have compassion for those less fortunate than himself. It was his duty.

But today hadn't been just about duty. Something about the very sick young girl had touched him in a way that he hadn't experienced in a very long time.

Maybe it was her stoic acceptance of death, and her strength in the face of all the hardship and injustices life had handed her. Or maybe it was because she was being struck down right on the cusp of womanhood—a time when she should be flirting and laughing with the village lads.

Or maybe it was because she reminded him of the older sister he'd lost to a fever a long time ago.

The two looked nothing alike—Annie was skinny, pale, and fair-haired, while Agnes had been dark, round, and brimming with vitality. But she'd been thirteen—probably a year or two younger than Annie—close enough to the same age to remind him.

Even after all these years, he still didn't like to think about it. He'd cared for his sister with a fierceness he'd never felt since—for anyone. So he pushed the memory aside, returning his attention to the woman beside him.

He could tell something was bothering her, but it wasn't until she stopped at the bottom of the stairs that he knew what it was.

"I owe you an apology."

Randolph stiffened, guessing what she wanted to apologize for. "It isn't necessary."

He had dismissed her accusations as soon as she'd made them—or at least as soon as his initial anger had a chance to cool down.

He knew how to laugh, damn it. He didn't take himself too seriously. And he sure as hell didn't always say what he thought people wanted to hear. She'd made him sound like a fraud—an *uptight* fraud, blast it.

It was only because her words were reminiscent of old accusations Erik "Hawk" MacSorley used to make that it had angered him at all. He'd been the butt of too many "poleaxes up the arse" jests from Hawk when they'd first fought together nearly eight years ago—right before Randolph made the biggest mistake of his life.

He'd given his vow of loyalty to his uncle Robert the Bruce, but after the English had found Randolph and some of Hawk's men on an island where they'd taken refuge, Randolph had switched allegiance. He'd been taken prisoner and hadn't had much choice in the matter—indeed, he'd escaped execution only because of his friendship with the Earl of Pembroke—but expedient or not, he'd broken his word.

The switch had been only temporary—and Hawk and the other members of the Highland Guard had made him pay for it ten times over in "training" when he'd returned—but the shame of the disloyalty to his uncle still haunted him.

But no one would ever question his word again. He was going to be the most loyal, most indispensable, most highly regarded knight in his uncle's retinue if it killed him. Everything was focused on that goal.

That's why her criticism had stung. Anger was the only reason why he'd been halfway up the stairs after Isabel to demand she retract what she'd said before he stopped himself.

Why would he care what Isabel Stewart thought? It

wasn't *her* approval he needed, it was her cousin's. *Elizabeth* was the one he was going to marry. Good thing, too, he thought. From what she'd said last night, Isabel was the type of woman who would make unrealistic demands, such as…

Loyalty. He frowned. Marriage was different. A certain freedom for men was expected. Elizabeth Douglas understood that, but instinctively he knew Isabel wouldn't.

One woman for the rest of his life? That wasn't for him. He knew some men did it, but they claimed to be "in love," which was as foreign a state as Randolph could imagine. He didn't get that attached. Incapable of feeling, she'd accused him? If she meant love—and in his experience, women always meant love—then she was right. That wasn't for him. He had no interest in those kinds of feelings. He was too focused on his goal: to be his uncle's greatest knight, lieutenant, and chief advisor. Randolph had let Bruce down once; he wasn't going to do it again. It was the only thing that mattered—nothing and no one would get in the way of that.

He started to turn away, but Isabel grabbed his arm to stop him. Christ, just the feel of her hand on him made his body jump.

"Yes, it is. I said some things…" She removed her hand from his arm, and he wasn't sure whether the self-conscious twisting of her hands and blush to her cheeks was for touching him, or for what she'd said last night. "I said some things that were wrong. I… I misjudged you, and I'm sorry. What you did in coming here was very kind." She gave him one of those wry smiles that he was beginning to find himself anticipating, almost looking forward to. He liked the way it made her eyes sparkle, her lips pull mischievously to one side, and a small dent appear in her cheek like a dimple. "I thought you were a little too good to be true."

He arched a brow. "And now?"

She laughed, batting long, thick eyelashes as if the light was too bright. "I'm properly dazzled right along with the rest of your admirers."

She was teasing him and didn't mean it, of course. She would never be like the others. She was different. Why the hell did that realization bother him so much?

"Are you ready, my lady?" The prioress had come into the hall behind them, and when they turned, she started. "I'm sorry, my lord, I did not realize you were helping us."

"He's not," Isabel interjected quickly. "The earl came to see Annie. He was just leaving."

"Helping with what?" he asked Isabel.

"A little work in the garden."

"I'm not as young as I once was," the prioress said. "It is hard work, and even with six of us, I was very grateful for Lady Isabel's help."

The prioress was seventy if she was a day. "Perhaps you could use another hand?" Randolph offered.

Before the prioress could respond, Isabel jumped in with something akin to alarm on her face. "That isn't necessary, my lord. I'm sure you are busy at the castle with the siege. We will manage fine." Then in a low voice that the aging prioress surely could not hear, she added, "Trust me, this is not something you will... uh... enjoy. The work is messy."

Did she think he'd never gotten dirty before? Or objected to a little manual labor every now and then? He wasn't uptight, damn it. She should have seen him digging pits and trenches for Hawk when he'd come back from England. The famed seafarer descended from Viking pirates had made Randolph eat his comment about not wanting to fight like a brigand in dirt.

He'd been lucky to be forgiven at all. His youth and the fact that he'd been taken prisoner had worked in his favor. Alex Seton, the former member of the Guard who'd turned traitor a couple of years ago, didn't have that excuse. Randolph pitied him if Hawk and the others ever got ahold of him.

Both his smile and spine were stiff as he turned to the prioress. "I insist. What do you need me to do?"

The prioress told him, and it took everything Randolph had not to mutter the curse that sprang to his lips.

The old nun had to be kidding! But she wasn't; he could tell by the way the woman at his side was trying not to laugh.

Isabel walked out of the hall and came back a minute later, carrying a pile of linen in her arms. "Here," she said, holding out what appeared to be an old apron. "You might want to wear this."

She wasn't smiling, but he could hear the laughter in her voice.

"That won't be necessary," he said tightly.

She shrugged. "Suit yourself. But that leather *cotun* won't be easy to clean, and the scent…"

"Izzie," he said darkly, cutting her off. If she was surprised by the use of the diminutive, she didn't show it.

She blinked up at him a little too innocently. "Yes?"

"Shut up." He marched outside, but not before starting to work the buckles of his *cotun*.

ISABEL WAS TRYING NOT TO laugh as she handed him the shovel—truly she was—but the jest possibilities were endless, including the one he made without intending to do so.

"This is what you volunteered to help with—shoveling shite?" he said incredulously, taking the implement from her.

She lifted a brow at his choice of words; dung or manure sounded much nicer. He had no idea the self-restraint she exercised to refrain from pointing out that surely "shoveling shite" was something he was used to.

But she didn't need to point it out; he read her thoughts easily enough, and his eyes narrowed to two piercing green daggers. His eyes turned very green when he was angry, she'd noticed. They were green a lot when he looked at her.

She might have been intimidated if she wasn't concentrating so hard on not bursting into laughter. The great Sir Thomas Randolph, Earl of Moray, in his shirtsleeves, slinging manure. What had she done to be so rewarded? She only wished she had an artist here to paint a picture so that she might immortalize the event forever.

"Don't blame me," she said with a mischievous grin. "I tried to warn you."

"Next time try harder—and mention the word fertilize."

She laughed and rolled her eyes. "Don't be such a bairn. There is no one here to see you toiling in the muck, and you certainly don't need to impress me. I know this doesn't have the glamor and shine of your usual heroic deeds, but it will all wash off, and you'll be all shimmery again in no time." She grinned. He must have realized she was teasing him because his jaw didn't lock and his mouth didn't pull into that familiar tight line. "Come, my lord, surely you know how to get a little dirty?"

"I know how to get plenty dirty but not in a garden."

Her brows drew together. She didn't understand. "My lord?"

He held her gaze and the hot, wicked look in his eyes led her to what he meant. Led her rather hotly and with far too many bodily twinges. Her stomach seemed to dance with a dip and a flip. Her cheeks flamed, and this time it was she who stiffened, pretending not to understand.

She heard him laugh when she turned and started on her own pile.

She couldn't say that she regretted his offer. With Randolph's help—especially with the tasks that required physical strength like lugging the carts back and forth to be filled in the barn and then returned to where they were working in the garden—the work that would have taken all day was finished in a matter of hours.

But it was more than that. Once the shock wore off, Randolph dove right in—to the job, not the dung—and took to the work with enthusiasm and zeal. He was a good laborer. The earl could proudly stand toe-to-toe with any farmer, ploughman, or villein. He didn't only know how to get dirty—she blushed recalling his earlier boast—he knew what he was doing. This wasn't the first time he'd fertilized a garden or done "menial" labor, and oddly the outdoor work suited him. When he put aside all the knightly bravado and perfection, she liked him. Maybe too much. The way her heart fluttered in his vicinity alarmed her. She almost wished she could go back to just seeing him as the larger-than-life legend in the making.

As the day progressed, he became noticeably more relaxed, jesting good-naturedly with the nuns, and even—she couldn't believe it—teasing her about her apron. "It's getting a little saturated." He sniffed. "Shall I fetch you a new one or have you grown used to the stench?"

She might have thrown something at him by accident. The clop of dirt—well, mostly dirt—landed right in the middle of his chest, but he didn't seem to care. He only laughed.

Blighter. She had told him that he didn't need to impress her, but she hadn't thought that she would care that he was seeing her looking so decidedly *un*glamorous. Not that she ever looked glamorous, but still!

That brought up one more reason why she didn't regret his offer to help. The view. It was spectacular. *He* was spectacular. Perhaps all those fawning admirers weren't so silly. She'd seen men in their shirtsleeves before but few—any?—could compare with the king's nephew. It was a warm day, and with the strenuous work, he got a little sweaty, and his shirt became a little damp and clingy, revealing the impressive bunches and bulges of muscle as he flexed. His chest was like a shield of steel—if there was fat anywhere she couldn't see it—and his arms…

Good gracious, his arms! They were sway-inducing, as she had discovered more than once. She felt a little light-headed every time he lifted something. Big and strong, they were the fodder of fantasies she didn't even know she had. Worse, she could recall too easily how they felt wrapped around her, holding *her* up.

Izzie knew she was in trouble. The amused indifference she'd felt toward her cousin's soon-to-be betrothed wasn't there anymore. It had started to change with that kiss, but had become far worse after today—first with Annie, and now seeing him like this.

But he wasn't for her—whether she could control her fluttering heart or not—nothing had changed about that. She needed to stay away from him if she didn't want to cause herself a lot of misery.

As soon as they were finished, she practically ran down to the large pond that was fed by the Leith River to wash as much of the muck off herself as she could. She would have to bathe, of course, but she could hardly go walking through town covered in shi—dung. She'd removed the stained apron and was kneeling on a large flat rock poised over the edge of the water trying to wash the worst off her face and hands when she sensed someone behind her.

She tensed, knowing who it was before she turned.

"Looks like we had the same idea," he said with a smile. "When I came back from returning the cart and you were gone, I thought you might have left."

Was she imagining the relief in his voice? Had he been disappointed to think she'd left without saying good-bye? God, she was a fool.

She plastered what she hoped was a careless smile on her face and said, "I thought I'd better wash the worst of it off before I returned to the abbey, or they might bar the door against me."

"Aye, even at camp where the stench is less than pleasant most of the time, I figured I'd better do the same."

He knelt beside her. The rock wasn't that big and his side brushed hers, as he washed his hands with the harsh efficiency she'd noticed of most soldiers and started to scoop water in his hands to splash over his face, not caring that he was getting his shirt wet.

It wasn't fair, she thought to herself. Even after a day of hard labor in the garden, covered in dirt and dung, he was gorgeous. Maybe even more gorgeous than usual. There was something primitively appealing about this physical side of him—the raw masculinity of a hot, sweaty man.

He didn't look so perfect, and she realized she liked it.

She liked him like this. *Like a man who knew how to get dirty.*

Her body flushed. She shouldn't think of that. It was dangerous. He was dangerous, and the intimacy of the situation certainly wasn't helping. They were alone in a secluded section of the garden, washing side-by-side. It would be fine if he were her brother or—her flush intensified—her husband.

It felt a little too natural, a little too perfect, and a little too much like they should be in a bedchamber. There was a sensual undercurrent in the air that made her heart flutter and her belly quiver. Did he feel it as well?

She needed to do something to lighten the mood. To dispel the aura of intimacy that made her imagine how easy it would be to do this every day, and how easy it would be to fall into his arms again.

Brother. What would she do if he were her brother?

A wicked smile turned her mouth. She dipped her hands into the water and looked at him. "I think you missed a spot."

As soon as he looked at her, she was ready. "I did?" he asked.

"Aye, right here." With as much force as she could, she pushed her hands through the water and splashed him in the face.

CHAPTER FIVE

THE DOUSING OF COLD WATER shocked the lust right out of him. Randolph had been struggling. He'd made the mistake of watching one stray drop of water make its way down her throat, to the bare skin above her bodice, and disappear between the deep cleft of her round breasts. He'd wanted to follow it with his tongue—wanted it with an intensity he didn't understand. He'd wanted to watch the water slide all over her body and lick the cool droplets from her flushed skin. Suck it from the tip of the tiny nipples that were beading through her dress from the chill of the water.

Those prickled nipples did him in. He'd turned as hard as a rock. Desire surged like a thunderbolt of fire through his blood.

He'd been trying not to think about how easy it would be to pull her into his arms again when she spoke. But when the water came barreling at him a moment later, he couldn't believe it. Bloody hell! She'd splashed him as if he were a lad of ten and not one of the most formidable knights in the land.

It wasn't indignation that roared through his blood, however. He wasn't just a knight; he was also a warrior. A *Highland* warrior whose first—only—instinct was to fight back and do what it took to win.

Shaking the water from his hair, he dipped his hands into the water. But the lass had obviously learned a thing or two from her always-fight-dirty Black Douglas cousin. Anticipating his retaliation, she put both her hands on him—

not in the place he ached for her to touch, unfortunately—
and gave him a big shove. Forward. Perched as he was on
the edge of the rocks, he only had one place to go: right into
the damned pond. A moment later he was covered in about
four feet of water that was marginally warmer than freeze-
your-bollocks-off cold.

The lass might not have realized it, but she'd just
declared war. And as one of Robert the Bruce's greatest
knights, he had no intention of losing. Before he surfaced, a
plan had already formed.

He stayed down at the silt bottom of the pond and didn't
come up for air. He was almost grateful for the training
(torture) he'd experienced at the hands of the Highland
Guard. Hawk had taken Randolph's change of allegiance
personally, and when he'd returned to the Bruce fold, he'd
spent over a month in the Western Isles under Hawk's
command—most of that time spent in the icy cold water of
the Irish Sea suffering and learning how to curse like a
seafarer. He'd been a passable swimmer when he'd started,
but by the time Hawk was done with him, Randolph could
swim for miles in the open ocean, stay afloat in the harshest
storm, and hold his breath underwater for four minutes—
Hawk could do over five.

Although he was out of practice, Randolph figured the
most he would need was three. But he'd barely counted to
two when the shadow appeared over him. As he'd expected,
she'd grown concerned that he couldn't swim and was
looking down into the water to see if he was all right.

He was ready. Moving too quickly for her to react, he
sprang from the water, grabbed her by the shoulders and
pulled her in.

The yelp of surprise would have become a scream if he
hadn't dragged her down under with him. Once he was sure
she was good and soaked, he brought them both up to the
surface.

The sound of laughter was the first thing he heard as she
twisted out of his hold and darted away from him. His hand
latched around a slim ankle. She tried to kick free—losing a

slipper in the effort, which he tossed back onto the rocks—but she was good and caught. Ignoring her laughing protests, he slowly wheeled her in.

Randolph couldn't remember the last time he'd had this much fun or felt so carefree. That he was doing so during the siege—the most important test he'd ever been given by Bruce—was even more remarkable.

Sliding one arm around her waist, he hauled her tight against his body. She wasn't getting away again; she was good and trapped in the ironclad bands of his arms. Every time she wriggled and pushed against his chest, his arms tightened. Their bodies were fused together, and even in the icy water he started to warm.

"Let go of me, you beast," she said, laughing. "That wasn't fair."

Her face tilted to his and he felt like he'd been clobbered in the head with a poleaxe. God, she was lovely. With her hair slicked back and water streaming down her face, the delicateness of her bone structure was more evident. Her beauty was timeless, he realized. The kind of beauty that became more pronounced the longer he looked at her. He could look at her a long time. *Maybe forever.*

Not knowing where that strange thought came from, he frowned and replied, "I hardly think you are in the position to cry foul, my lady. I wasn't the one who started it. First rule of combat is don't start a war you can't win."

She huffed with obvious affront. "I had every intention of winning until you tricked me. Really, my lord, playing on my sympathy by pretending to be drowning? That is hardly the height of chivalry. What would your legions say?"

He gave her a devilish grin. "My legions would say I won."

She tossed her head back and laughed, and he felt something hard squeezing his chest. *So damned beautiful.*

Perhaps the sudden coiled tension in his body alerted her. She stopped laughing and her eyes met his in… question? Longing? Desire?

Maybe all those things and more. But whatever it was, the mood went from playful to something else in an instant. Something hot and fiery and powerful enough to make him forget the cold and all the reasons why he shouldn't touch her again.

Touching her, kissing her, seemed the most natural thing ever.

So he did. But the passion took him by surprise. It burst through him at contact and barreled forward with the force of a rock slung from a trebuchet—there was no stopping it. One minute he was kissing her, and the next his hands were all over her body, and he was out of control. Which didn't make any sense, since he didn't *get* out of control. But he had become mad with pleasure, frenzied with lust, and ravenous with a hunger that would only be satisfied one way.

IZZIE WASN'T COLD ANYMORE. HOW could she be when she had his heat to warm her? His mouth, his tongue, his hands. My lord his hands! They were incredible. Big, strong, and possessive, yet warm and surprisingly gentle, they were on her bottom, her hips, her breasts. She didn't know a man's touch could do this to her. Turn her into a tangled, coiled mass of desire and need.

When his hands cupped and squeezed her breasts, her back arched for more. More pressure, more friction, more of his thumb rubbing over the throbbing tip.

It felt so good. She had no idea her breasts were so sensitive.

She moaned her pleasure, and he broke the kiss with a curse. She missed the heat of his mouth and tongue instantly—desperately. But then it was replaced with an even hotter fire as his mouth slid down her throat, over the exposed part of her chest, and then—oh my lord in heaven—over her breast as he tugged the fabric down enough to free her nipple.

The heat of his mouth was wondrous. She gave a soft cry of pleasure and arched deeper against him. His tongue went to work, teasing her at first with gentle circles and flicks, and then when he had her squirming and moaning, increasing the friction by drawing her slowly between his teeth, and finally, when she didn't think she could stand it anymore, sucking her deep into his mouth.

She cried out at the incredible sensations. At the needles of pleasure that pulled between her breasts and the intimate place between her legs that felt so restless and quivery. That seemed to crave friction. Instinctively, her hips started to move against the solid length of his manhood.

She must have been doing something right because he made a harsh sound and sucked her harder, increasing her frustration and turning her into a throbbing pool of need. When she finally felt something brush against that secret place, she was so poised on the edge, it took her a moment to realize it was his hand. No, his fingers. Caressing, teasing, and finally—oh God, yes *that*—slipping inside her.

Her entire body shuddered. Shock and wonder collided in an explosion of new, intense sensations that flooded her with heat. Mirroring the rhythmic flicks of his tongue on her nipple, his finger stroked between her legs. Vaguely she realized that she should probably be embarrassed by the way he was touching her, but it simply felt too good. Her wantonness would mortify her later.

Whatever he was doing to her, she had no ability to resist. His reputation was well earned. He knew exactly what to do to bring her pleasure. Her body was like an instrument and he played it expertly, bringing her to a violent crescendo. He made the sensations build and build until they had nowhere to go.

Her body clenched, straining toward the final peak, and then finally soared into a realm of sensation that was indescribable. She felt transported—separated from her body as if she'd died for a moment—glimpsed heaven, and then came slowly back to earth in a shattering explosion of floating, spasming waves.

The waves had barely ebbed when he picked her up and carried her out of the water. A moment later, she was down on the grass and he was kissing her again. This time with a tenderness and a sweetness that made her heart break.

Nay, not break, she realized, *open*. She was falling hard and fast for Sir Thomas Randolph, and she feared there was nothing she could do to stop it. *What's not to love?* She'd better figure out something quick.

THERE WAS NOTHING RANDOLPH LOVED more than to bring a woman pleasure. He loved the euphoria that transformed their features into something almost heavenly, he loved the pink flush that rose to their cheeks, the way their lips parted, their eyes closed, and their heads fell back as their bodies gave over in that final surrender. It was a look he'd seen many, many times before, and it always brought him a deep sense of satisfaction.

But that was nothing compared to the fierce, primal feelings pounding through him now. He felt satisfaction, aye, but it was far deeper, far stronger, and far more primitive in its intensity than the vaguely detached feelings he'd experienced before. There was nothing detached about his feelings right now. He was experiencing every gasp, every clench, every spasm of pleasure right along with her. Her pleasure seemed integral—bound—to his own.

He didn't understand it, and he wasn't sure he liked it. It was different, and he rather liked the way things were. His relations with women had always been easy. Something he didn't have to think about. They liked him and he liked them. Simple. But what he felt right now sure as hell wasn't simple. It was powerful, demanding, and intense. It was hunger and desire to the extreme.

Her breasts hadn't helped. Who the hell would have guessed she hid such perfection under all those modest gowns? They were spectacular. About the most spectacular he'd ever seen. The round shape, the more than a handful size, the creamy velvet of her porcelain skin, and the delicate shade of pink of those taut little nipples. He would dream about those nipples. How sweet they'd tasted, how they'd felt rolling under his tongue, how much he'd like to feel them raking against his chest as he moved in and out of her.

Aye, he'd like that a lot—especially the moving in and out part. He wanted to be inside her. Wanted it with a desperate ache that he hadn't experienced in a long time. Maybe ever. Which didn't make sense. But he was beyond sense.

It was her response that undid him. The moans, the little arches of her back that begged for more. He knew he could make her shatter, and once that knowledge was lodged in his head he couldn't let it go. He had to touch her. Had to stroke her. Had to feel her release as he brought her to completion.

He just hadn't anticipated the effect it would have on *him*.

His body was still hard as a rock, and lust pounded at the base of his spine, but his chest... his chest seemed to expand and fill with warmth and an overwhelming sense of pleasure. Not physical pleasure, but a deep, overwhelming sense of contentment—almost joy. The pain in his body—which hurt like hell—seemed secondary. He wanted to be inside her more than he'd ever wanted with any other woman, but he also wanted to snuggle her against his chest and hold her tight.

It was the damnedest thing, and he didn't know what the hell to make of it.

Randolph wasn't a man who was controlled by his lust, but when he carried her out of the water and caught a glimpse of the long, sleek limbs now visible beneath her sodden gown, he reconsidered. He might have forgotten every last ounce of his honor and taken her right there, if he hadn't looked down at her face.

She looked so incredibly beautiful—and very sweet and trusting. His chest squeezed as a hot swell of an unfamiliar emotion rose up inside him. It was the same strange feeling that made him want to hold her against his chest and protect her.

Protect her.

The realization did what the cold water had not, cooling the heat from his blood. He couldn't do this. He had to stop. It was wrong even if nothing had ever felt more right. He couldn't take her innocence no matter how hard his body urged it. She wasn't his, and doing this wouldn't make her so. He'd given his word. He wouldn't back out of the planned betrothal with Elizabeth just because her cousin made him out of his mind with lust.

So instead of ravishing her senseless as every fiber of his body urged to do, he kissed her gently. Tenderly. Telling her in a way that words could not how much what had just happened meant to him.

It *had* meant something to him, he realized. Though what, he wasn't sure. Nor did he like it. But whatever it was, it didn't make a difference.

Reluctantly, he lifted his head and gently stroked a wet lock of fair hair from her brow. Her pale skin was like velvet, and his thumb lingered on the delicate bones of her cheek as if he could hold on to the moment for just a little longer.

Even though he knew it had to end.

IZZIE COULD TELL BY THE WAY he was looking at her that something had changed. *Regret.* That's what she read in his eyes, and it cast a sudden shadow over what might have been the most wonderful moment of her life. For the briefest instant—not much more than the space of a heartbeat—when his lips had caressed hers so tenderly, so lovingly, she'd felt that she wasn't alone. She'd felt as if the same strange emotions that were confusing her might be confusing him, too. That maybe—just maybe—he might be falling for her, too.

She'd felt the possibility of something wonderful. Something special. Something that might be meaningful. But now that feeling was slipping away.

"What's wrong?" she asked.

His brows drew together in a slight frown. "Nothing."

"Then why did you stop?" Her cheeks heated as she realized the boldness of what she'd said.

She sat up, no longer feeling comfortable lying on the ground with him stretched out half on top of her. Though a moment ago she'd thought being under him the most natural place in the world.

He followed suit, and without the closeness, without the connection, without his heat, she was suddenly cold. She drew her knees in tight against her chest and wrapped her arms around them, unconsciously perhaps protecting herself against what he was about to say.

He bent one knee and looked idly at the pond, his thoughts inscrutable. He must be freezing as well, but he gave no hint of it. Feelings, emotions, cold... he looked like a man impervious to anything so plebeian. "Because if I went any further, honor would demand that I ask for your hand."

The stab between her ribs was surprisingly sharp. She understood. "And you don't want that."

He gave her a sharp look as if her words had pricked. "I'm practically engaged to your cousin."

"Practically," she said. "But not actually."

She hadn't meant it as a challenge, but he seemed to take it as such. Some of the stiffness and defensiveness that had been absent for most of the day returned. "It's the same thing. I gave my word to Douglas that I would offer for his sister, and I can't go back on it."

"Can't or won't?" She couldn't believe she was talking to him like this—about this—but somehow she knew if she didn't say something now, it might be too late. It had suddenly become imperative that he not become betrothed to her cousin. Whatever possibility she'd felt in something wonderful would be gone.

His mouth pressed in a tight line. "Both."

Izzie had never lacked for confidence, but even she was surprised when she said, "Even if you want me?"

He didn't deny it, but neither from the way he shrugged did it seem overly important to him. Maybe it wasn't. Maybe she'd just imagined something that wasn't there. Maybe it didn't mean anything. Maybe what she'd felt had been one-sided. Maybe for him it was no more than desire. Lust. Something he was used to.

He did this all the time. She knew that women loved him. Flocked to him. Shame heated her cheeks. *Offered* themselves to him. Why should Izzie think she was any different?

Why would he care about someone like her? He was extraordinary, and she was... not.

Just look at him. He had everything. He was a knight at the peak of his prowess, gorgeous beyond reckoning with his dark hair, piercing greenish-brown eyes, and too-handsome features; he was one of the wealthiest men in the kingdom, the favored nephew of the king, and a legend in the making with his fantastic feats on the battlefield. If she'd written a faerie tale she couldn't have come up with a more unbelievably perfect hero.

Of course women loved him. But they didn't see what she saw. They didn't see the real man underneath. The man who could be dry and sarcastic, who could sing like an angel one moment and be as devious as the Devil the next (she was determined to get him back for tricking her into leaning over the pond), who shared her interest in architecture and could hold her spellbound while talking about rocks—right before he heroically saved her life from an avalanche of them. The man who was driven to be the best, and yet had time to help nuns fertilize their garden and make a dying young peasant girl feel like a princess. She could admire the hero like everyone else, but that was the man whom she could love.

"I see," she said and started to stand up.

He grabbed hold of her arm, his hand wrapping around her wrist like a brand. "No, you don't." His sudden fierceness made her think maybe he wasn't as uncaring and ambivalent as he seemed. "I gave my word, Izzie. My *word*."

Was that supposed to make her understand? Because if so, it wasn't working. She suddenly felt like crying. "You said that."

"I will not go back on it again—ever."

"I didn't ask you to."

"But that's what you want."

It wasn't a question, so she didn't say anything. Is that what she wanted? Maybe it was. Maybe she wanted him to choose her—as unlikely as that may be.

She tugged at her arm, and he let her go without a fight.

That seemed somehow telling.

She was shivering now; her lips were probably a pale shade of violet. All she could think about was getting back to the abbey and trying to forget about this. Trying to forget about him. She just hoped she didn't burst into tears before she got there. Her pride had taken enough of a battering for the day.

What could she have been thinking? This was *Randolph*. He wanted great and extraordinary; he wouldn't tie himself to someone who wouldn't enhance his image. Someone who loved court and would be an asset to his ambitions. That wasn't her.

She looked around for her cloak, glad that she'd left it on a fallen tree while she'd washed. But the warmth that enfolded her was temporary.

She felt like such a fool. She'd practically handed him her innocence because she thought a few heated moments and tender kisses meant something. No matter how kind, how fun, how attached he'd seemed, how could she have let herself believe even for one minute that she was the kind of woman to capture the heart of a lauded rogue? Rogues didn't fall for one woman. That's what made them rogues. And if there was *a* woman who would ever bring him to heel, it would be a glittery diamond to add to his crown, like her cousin.

Her chest squeezed. Izzie wasn't a diamond. She probably wasn't even a pearl. She was just the not-so-glamorous cousin—the supporting player to the lead in this faerie tale. The one who didn't get the happy ending.

She made it to the edge of the trees before he spoke. "I could never give you what you want, Izzie—even without Elizabeth."

She felt the first stirrings of anger. Did he think she was already in love with him? His arrogance truly was astounding—even if he was closer than she wanted to acknowledge. She spun around, fists balled tightly at her side. "I don't want anything from you."

"Good, because I could never give it. You were right—I don't have those kinds of feelings. You want someone who cares for you."

She'd thought the pang in her heart couldn't sink any deeper, but he'd just proved her wrong. "And you don't," she said, saying what he hadn't.

"Not in the way you want."

She felt the lash of truth like a lick of flame. He'd left no room for misinterpretation, had he? He might as well have said, "I don't love you, nor shall I."

She wouldn't let him see how much his honesty had hurt her. She drew herself up, meeting his gaze unflinchingly. "And my cousin? Does she deserve that as well? Or maybe you care for her already?"

He bristled, not seeming to like her point. "Your cousin and I understand one another."

In other words, her cousin wouldn't make demands because she wouldn't be fool enough to fall in love with him. Izzie gave him a pitying look. At times he could truly be an arse. "How fortunate for you. It sounds perfect. And that is what you want, isn't it?"

She wasn't expecting an answer. Without another word, or another look in his direction, she left.

What else could she do? He'd made himself clear. He didn't care for her; he wouldn't love her; and he wasn't going to call off his betrothal.

He'd said everything he needed to say.

CHAPTER SIX

RANDOLPH HID HIS SURPRISE WHEN he saw Lady Isabel coming out of the guesthouse behind her cousin. He'd assumed that she would beg off from the outing to the market that had been arranged a few days ago.

But he should have known better. Isabel—Izzie—wasn't one to beg off anything. She confronted—whether the situation was comfortable or not.

In this case, it was not.

His discomfort wasn't because of anything she was doing. Rather the opposite. Although her gaze had flickered to his on greeting, she paid little attention to him the rest of the morning and seemed to be enjoying the outing with her cousin.

She gave no hint of the intense conversation they'd had yesterday—or of the intimacies they'd shared, for that matter. She was her usual confident, self-possessed, lighthearted, wryly funny, annoyingly indifferent-to-him self. His jaw clenched as he watched Isabel and her cousin laugh with some merchant over the cost of his ribbons. No one in the crowd who was watching them (they'd drawn a lot of attention from the townsfolk) would ever guess that she'd fallen apart in his arms.

That she'd given herself to him.

But he knew, damn it. And every time he looked at her, every time he heard her laugh at something Elizabeth said, every time she took a big bite out of one of those flaky fruit tarts she loved so much, he thought about it. He'd nearly done something more than think when the juice from one of the berry tarts dribbled down the side of her mouth. He'd been a hair's breadth from reaching down to swipe it away from her lips with his finger—or his tongue, he couldn't decide which.

Bloody hell. The lass was tormenting him, and didn't even know it.

She, on the other hand, treated him if not as a stranger, then with the polite formality due the intended of her cousin.

That was exactly what he wanted. Which didn't explain his irritation or the feeling that his armor was suddenly too tight every time he looked at her—which was too damned often!

It was only his conscience bothering him, he told himself. He hadn't meant to hurt her; he'd just wanted to make sure there was no... *confusion.*

He'd seen that look in her eyes and knew what she was thinking. God knows he'd seen it enough times to recognize it. She'd thought something "special" was happening. That what they'd had was "different." That she was falling in love with him. She'd probably been dreaming of castles in the skies, a handful of children around their feet with a few damned pups thrown in. He was hardly the type for sitting around the hearth; he liked excitement—and variety, for that matter.

But it was just the passion confusing her. Hell, he ought to know. For a few minutes there even he'd been feeling a little confused—and he wasn't a twenty-two-year-old lass being touched for the first time, he was a twenty-nine-year-old experienced knight who should know better.

Not for you. You gave your word.

"Is something wrong with the collar of your mail?" Elizabeth asked. "You keep tugging at it."

Randolph dropped his hand, feeling oddly self-conscious as Isabel's gaze landed on him for the first time in too-damned long. "My coif was a little stuck, that's all," he said, hoping the explanation didn't sound as silly as he felt.

"I'm afraid I am no help with that. I have little experience with a knight's armor. Maybe Izzie can help? She has seven brothers, after all."

"Nay!"

"No!"

Randolph didn't know whose protest came quicker—or louder. Elizabeth looked back and forth between him and Izzie questioningly, but thankfully, not suspiciously.

She must not have noticed Izzie's flush. But he had. It was the first crack in her facade; the first indication that she hadn't completely forgotten what had happened yesterday. But it wasn't the biggest. That had come with the bracelet.

What the hell had possessed him to buy a bracelet for Lady Elizabeth with Izzie standing there? He knew very well what it signified. A man only bought jewelry for a woman he was married to or intended to marry.

But he'd been feeling reckless, angry, pushed to the edge by her indifference and whatever the hell other emotion was eating at him relentlessly.

She wasn't even looking at him, but he felt like she was pulling at him, asking him to do something he didn't want to do. He *couldn't* do, damn it. She was putting too much stock in a little attraction. They barely knew one another. He was supposed to break his word and put aside a lucrative alliance because he couldn't keep his hands off her? It was unrealistic—ridiculous even. This attraction would pass. It always did. Even if this was a little stronger than usual.

He sure as hell wasn't in love with her. Nor did he have any intention of falling over that particular cliff. He shuddered at the thought. He'd seen the signs enough to know. Hell, most of the men he fought with in Bruce's Guard had succumbed to "love" and the idiocy that went along with it. At least they'd all acted like idiots while they were courting their wives. They stopped looking at other women, they became overprotective and fiercely possessive if anyone looked at *their* woman, they acted irrationally and crazily—alternatively miserable and overly happy depending on whether the lass looked at them the right way.

They forgot their honor by anticipating the wedding night, and once they'd "won" their prize they walked around with a ridiculous "I'm the luckiest bastard in the world" grin on their faces.

He wasn't doing any of that. Why he'd looked at another woman just the other day, right before... Izzie and her cousin arrived. His mouth fell in a grim line. That didn't mean anything. He wasn't being irrational or possessive—although if that one tart merchant had looked at her chest any longer, he would have felt the edge of Randolph's sword. It was his duty, that was all. That he didn't feel the need to defend Elizabeth's honor—who'd had a good number of looks at her chest as well—didn't mean anything.

None of it meant anything. He was just a little distracted, that's all. He needed to focus on the prize.

So he'd made his intentions clear with the bracelet.

But he hadn't meant to hurt Isabel. And though there was nothing in her eyes—no condemnation, no betrayal, no anything—when their gazes met, he knew he had.

He wanted to apologize, but when he tried to pull her to the side after he'd been called back to camp—the Highland Guard had returned from a mission—she wouldn't let him.

Knowing he had to go, he vowed to try later, while doing his best to prove to everyone—including himself—that the betrothal with Elizabeth was what he wanted.

Of course it was. Elizabeth was perfect.

Perfect. *"That is what you want, isn't it?"* He could still hear the taunt in Izzie's voice. Aye, and he would have it. Everything was going to be perfect, damn it. Tomorrow he would get it over— He stopped, correcting himself. Tomorrow he would propose to Elizabeth.

As much as he wanted to apologize to Izzie, it was probably better for them both if he stayed away.

But later, when he returned to his tent to wash and saw the package that was waiting for him, he smiled. He'd almost forgotten that he'd sent his squire on a hunt for it. Maybe there was something he could do to apologize, after all.

≪

INSENSITIVE...UNFEELING...LOUT! How could he buy her cousin such a meaningful gift with her standing right there? Maybe Izzie had been right in her estimation of him from the start. Maybe Randolph was incapable of genuine feelings and emotion, and yesterday was an aberration. She'd felt as if she'd been on a stage all morning with the crowd watching them, and his brilliant performance as the perfect—she was really beginning to hate that word—doting suitor.

But the purchase of the beautiful bracelet had been just as much for Izzie as it had been for the crowd. He was making a statement—which wasn't necessary. She'd heard him well enough the first time.

Stupid, stupid, stupid! Her anger wasn't just for him; it was directed at herself as well. She knew better, and still she'd let herself think that the passion between them meant something. It meant something all right. It meant that she was a naive fool, and if he hadn't put a stop to it, she would have been a naive *ruined* fool. She supposed she had to thank him for that at least. It hadn't been a complete seduction.

But it had been enough. The way he'd touched her, the way he'd made her feel, the way he'd looked into her eyes...

She cursed and forced her thoughts away. She couldn't think about it. She would never think about it again. She'd seen only what she wanted to see.

"Did you say something, Izzie?" Elizabeth asked.

Izzie bit her lip and winced, realizing that she must have muttered her curse aloud. She and her cousin were returning to the guesthouse after the midday meal. They were both unusually quiet and lost in thought, although Izzie could guess what her cousin was thinking about. She'd seen Elizabeth's face when Thom MacGowan had left the refectory with the newly arrived Lady Marjorie Rutherford, a widowed baroness who'd made it clear she did not object to the son of a blacksmith turned man-at-arms for a husband. If he'd been a bowl of cream, the young widow would have been lapping him up the entire meal.

If Izzie hadn't been sure before, watching Elizabeth trying to hide her panic and jealousy during the long meal had made it absolutely clear: her cousin loved Thom MacGowan. Not that it would change anything. The public censure from such an unequal match—even if Randolph weren't involved—would be horrible. Izzie wasn't sure she would have the strength to withstand it, and she hadn't had the difficult past that Elizabeth had.

With Randolph involved, it would be even worse: there would also be a scandal. Setting aside a "prince" for a "peasant"… it would be the talk for years—and not the kind of talk Randolph was eager for. She could just imagine his reaction. She'd see some real emotion from him then. But anger, rage, and humiliation weren't what she wanted.

She wanted…

Her chest squeezed, and she pushed it away. *Stupid.*

"Sorry," Izzie apologized, shaking it off. "I was just talking to myself again."

"Is something upsetting you, cousin? You've been quiet since we returned from the market." Elizabeth frowned. "Did Randolph say something to irritate you again? I heard him trying to apologize for something before he left. I'd hoped that you would grow to like him better once you got to know him."

Izzie felt another tug. Mission accomplished. "What's not to love," she said with an attempt at lightheartedness, repeating her cousin's much-loved jest about Randolph. But it didn't sound very funny to her anymore. "He stepped on my foot," she added quickly. "And was apologizing for crushing my toes with his boot."

Toes… heart, what was the difference?

Elizabeth smiled, but Izzie could tell she was still upset.

Joanna was waiting for them when they arrived back at the guesthouse. When she asked Elizabeth if she could take care of an errand for her, from the way her cousin suddenly perked up, Izzie didn't need to guess who that errand involved.

Elizabeth looked so happy that for one selfish moment, Izzie was tempted to say something about Randolph. Undoubtedly Izzie's feelings would be the excuse Elizabeth needed to follow her heart. But as Izzie wasn't even sure that was what she thought her cousin should do, she kept her mouth shut.

But that wasn't the only reason. Izzie had her pride. She didn't want to be second choice. If Randolph wanted her—if he did care about her—he would pick her first. It was silly and unrealistic to expect maybe, but she wouldn't settle for less.

Still, she couldn't help warning her cousin as she left with Joanna. "Have care, El." She paused. "Be sure what you want before you do something you can't take back."

Izzie didn't know whether she meant doing something irreversible with Thom (like Izzie had nearly done yesterday with Randolph) or irreversible with Randolph by accepting his proposal. Maybe she meant both.

Elizabeth caught her gaze and didn't pretend to not understand. She nodded soberly and went after Joanna. It was Joanna who turned just as they were out the door. "Oh Izzie, I forgot to tell you. One of the monks brought a package for you. I had the maid leave it in your room."

Izzie's surprise showed. "A package?"

Jo smiled and waggled her brows. "Perhaps you have a secret admirer you haven't told us about?"

With a wry grin, Izzie shook her head. "I'm afraid nothing so exciting. It's probably the woolen hose I ordered from the haberdasher."

They were both wrong.

When Izzie unwrapped the leather bound codex a few minutes later, she thought her heart would squeeze out of her chest, as she ran her fingers slowly—longingly—over the gold embossed letters: *Naturalis Historia.*

Randolph had found the book for her.

She felt the emotion rising in her chest to her throat and

pushed it back. Why was he doing this? Why was he torturing her? Was he trying to make her fall in love with him or hate him? She didn't want thoughtfulness and kindness—not if he was going to marry her cousin. But how could he give her something like this and claim it didn't mean anything? Was it some kind of apology? Some kind of gift to allay his guilt?

Neither was acceptable. She wasn't going to let him off that easily.

But before she could think exactly how to return the book to him—she could hardly go marching into a siege camp... or could she?—a message arrived from St. Mary's.

IT WAS ALMOST TIME FOR the evening meal when Izzie returned to Holyrood from the hospital, but she didn't feel much like eating. Nor did she feel much like talking to anyone, so she sought out her favorite corner in the small garden, where she could just sit and stare at the plants and flowers and let the sense of peace enfold her.

It didn't work. She could not seem to stop the occasional tear from slipping beneath her red-rimmed eyes.

"Izzie."

Her breath caught at the sound of his voice. She turned to see Randolph standing at the gate with his helm tucked under his arm, looking as if he'd run straight from the battlefield. Both his mail and surcoat were stained with mud, and streaks of sweat were still visible on his face in the sandy light of dusk.

He must have seen the tears in her eyes because he said, "You know."

"That Annie died?" She nodded. "Aye, I just returned from the hospital a few minutes ago." Her throat was thick, and a fresh stream of tears threatened, but she held them back. It seemed silly that she was this upset by someone she barely knew. But something about the young girl had touched her—touched them both.

Randolph took a seat beside her and took her icy hand in his. She let him, too numb to protest or ascribe meaning.

"There was a message from the prioress when I returned to my tent," he explained. "I'd hoped it had just arrived so that I could be the one to tell you."

"You didn't go to the hospital?"

He frowned. "Nay, I came here first."

His first instinct had been to find her. That had to mean something. "How did you find me in the garden?"

He shrugged. "You mentioned you liked to come out here to read sometimes. I took a chance on my way to the guesthouse when I didn't see you in the Hall."

She'd mentioned it once—only briefly—but he'd remembered. "My cousin prefers the south garden—it is larger with more trees."

Elizabeth had mentioned it in the same conversation.

"Does she? You said you liked the flowers."

Don't read too much into it. But how could she not?

"You shouldn't be out here alone; it will be dark soon," Randolph said.

A slight rueful smile broke through the sadness. "It's an abbey, my lord, I think any threat to my safety is small."

His face darkened ever so slightly. "There are still soldiers about."

Apparently, he was serious. She'd never thought of him as the overprotective type.

She shifted her gaze to her lap. To the big hand still wrapped so tenderly around hers. "I shall endeavor to be more careful in the future."

If he heard her sarcasm, he chose to ignore it. "I'm sorry, Izzie." He gave her hand a squeeze. "I know you cared for the lass. Even though Helen had prepared me, it still came as a shock."

Izzie nodded. "She seemed so happy yesterday." So *alive*.

"Surely that is a good thing. Her last day on earth was a happy one to prepare her for a better future."

Izzie wanted to believe that, but tears filled her eyes. "It just feels so wrong."

Perhaps he realized how close to tears she was because he drew her into his arms to comfort her. And it did—he did. The peace that had eluded her before settled over her like a soft, warm plaid. A soft warm plaid that held the faint hint of cinnamon and leather.

"It is wrong," he said gravely. "It feels like that whenever someone so young passes."

There was something in his voice that made her look up at him, as if she knew there was more.

He wiped a tear from her eye, the thumb callused from years of sword fighting achingly gentle. Their eyes met and the pull was nearly overwhelming. Her chest squeezed with something akin to longing. *I could love him.* It would be so easy to let herself succumb to what felt so right.

What he saw in her gaze must have encouraged him. His voice cracked as if the words were hard to get out. "My older sister died when she was thirteen."

She hadn't realized... she'd thought he was an only child. "How old were you?"

"Eight. It was right before I was sent out to be fostered. I remember being grateful that I'd had the time with her, and that it hadn't happened when I was gone."

Izzie had seven brothers. They drove her crazy with their antics most of the time, but she loved them dearly and couldn't imagine losing any one of them. She knew she was lucky—it was rare to have so many of them escape the cruel reaper of childhood.

Her heart went out to him. "I'm sorry," she said and put her hand on his arm.

He looked down on it for a long moment—as if her touch meant something—before meeting her gaze again. His mouth curved on one side. "It was a long time ago."

"But you loved her very much."

His arms squeezed around her a little tighter. She wondered if he even noticed?

"Aye. I did."

Strangely, in the midst of tragedy, the easy admission

filled her with hope. If he'd had the capacity to love before, he could do so again. Indeed, she wondered if he did a little already. She wasn't alone in this—whatever *this* was—she wasn't.

"Why did you really come here, Thomas?"

She'd never called him by his given name before, but she didn't think he noticed. He drew back and let her fall out of the comfort of his embrace. "I already told you. I heard the wee lass had passed on."

"Then why didn't you go to the hospital?"

He stared at her mutely, not understanding the implication. She wondered if it might be intentional.

"Why did you send me the book?" she persisted, willing him to see it.

"I wanted to apologize for earlier at the market."

The bracelet. It was what she had initially thought, but now she wondered. "Did you find it in one of the shops on high street at the market today?"

His gaze turned slightly askew. "Nay, I had my squire hunting for it the past few days. He found it at a local priory."

"I see. So it wasn't an apology then. Or did you anticipate doing something cruel and needing to apologize for it a few days ago?"

He stiffened. "I didn't do anything cruel."

"Didn't you?"

"It was just a bracelet," he said defensively. "It didn't mean anything."

They both knew that wasn't quite true. He'd known what it would mean to Izzie.

"You don't owe me any explanations, my lord."

"We are back to my lord? You called me Thomas before."

He *had* noticed. She didn't say anything. But maybe the way she looked at him said enough.

He tore his gaze from hers, made a sound of frustration, and stood from the bench as he raked his fingers through his hair. Even crimped from the helm and clumped with sweat, it fell in dark shimmery waves to his chiseled jawline. Did he ever look less than stomach-droppingly gorgeous? When she probably had puffy, red eyes and blotchy skin. Truly, it wasn't fair.

"I told you how it is."

"Aye, you gave your word to Jamie and won't go back on it."

Again. That was what he'd said before. Had he given his word in the past and broken it? Was that what this was about?

His next words seemed to suggest so. "Do you know what people would say? How it would look? I won't have my honor—my loyalty—brought into question."

Loyalty? It was an odd word choice for a proposed betrothal, but suddenly why this was so important to him made sense. "You don't want to remind anyone of what you did by switching sides to fight with the English."

His lips pressed together until the muscle in his jaw began to tic. She wasn't sure whether his anger was at being reminded of his dishonorable past or the fact that she'd guessed his reasons. Maybe it was both.

Though his stony expression looked impenetrable, she had to try. There wasn't time to wait for him to see the truth. By then he could be engaged, and breaking a betrothal *was* a serious matter. In a strange way Annie's death gave her the courage to be bold. To reach for what she wanted. God knew, life could be preciously short.

"You've made up for what you did back then tenfold since you've returned. No one questions your loyalty. You are one of the king's most important and respected knights."

His eyes seemed to shine as dark as onyx in the fading light. "Because I've kept my word—and I intend to keep it that way. But people remember. *I* remember, damn it."

The fierceness of his response took her aback. She could practically feel it radiating from him and hear the lingering shame in his voice. This was what drove him. This was what had made him so intent on becoming the perfect knight who could do no wrong and who everyone admired.

It made an odd kind of sense. "You don't need to be perfect; no one is going to criticize you."

She didn't think it possible, but his mouth hardened even more. "That's right. They aren't. Because I will not give them a reason to."

Izzie felt her frustration—and not an insignificant amount of anger—rise inside her. He was being ridiculous! Not to mention stubborn. If he'd ever needed to prove himself to anyone, he didn't any longer. He was a hero already and on his way to becoming a legend. But men and their honor—*Highlanders* and their honor, she corrected—could be as intractable as mules and as dogmatic as inquisitors.

She stood to face him; her hands fisted into tight balls at her side. "So you will marry my cousin and you will both be miserable, but it won't matter because you didn't break your word to Jamie, is that it?"

Her voice made it clear how asinine she thought that was—which he just as clearly did not appreciate. God, she hated when he retracted into the stiff, arrogant, I-can-do-no-wrong knight.

His eyes narrowed to suspicious slits. "What makes you think we will be miserable?"

She wasn't going to be the one to tell him about Elizabeth. "You would see it if you stopped worrying about what everyone else thinks and look at what is right in front of you."

He took her by an arm and hauled her against him. The heat of his body was like a spark of wildfire to her senses setting them aflame.

"What the Devil is that supposed to mean?" he growled.

She lifted her chin, refusing to be intimidated or put off by his anger. "It means that I think you are too stubborn and convinced that you aren't capable of caring about someone to see that you do."

"Who?" He dragged her closer with a sneer. "You?"

But he wasn't as unaffected as he wanted her to think. His nostrils flared when the contact made her nipples harden against him. She could practically feel the attraction firing in the air between them. She gave him a look that dared him to deny this. "Aye, me."

Choose me.

He made another growl of frustration and pulled her in even closer. He wanted to kiss her. She could see it. Feel it. Every muscle in his body seemed to be straining with the effort of holding himself back.

Her heart squeezed. For a moment she thought he would break. That he would give in to this… in to them.

But he didn't. Instead, he set her purposefully away from him. "You are wrong. I have no intention of falling in love with you—or anyone else for that matter."

Maybe she was wrong. Maybe she was just seeing what she wanted to see.

But when he walked away, Izzie realized that whether she was right or wrong no longer mattered. He was going to choose her cousin, and the door that had opened in her heart would slam closed. Although if the heavy darkness that weighed upon her chest was any indication, it might already have.

CHAPTER SEVEN

RANDOLPH COULD SEE JUST FINE. He knew exactly what he was doing. *"Both be miserable…"* He scoffed. Whatever the hell Izzie thought she knew, she was wrong. His fists clenched as he stormed through the abbey gate in search of Douglas. He was perfectly content, damn it.

The fact that he'd been up most of the night pacing the very small floor space of his tent—nearly tripping over his page and squire a dozen times—and wanting to put his fist through a wall, didn't mean anything. He was angry, that was all. *Irritated.*

She was the one who was being ridiculous. He was supposed to put aside his plans and break his word because she claimed to see something he couldn't? After a handful of days, Isabel Stewart knew him better than he knew himself? And why was she so certain that he cared about her? Because they shared a few unusual interests? Because the passion between them was explosive and made him do things—nearly taking her innocence for one—that he'd never done before? Because every time he looked at her, he thought about how she'd looked coming apart in his arms, and he wanted to see it again and again? Because she made him laugh a few times and relax more than he had in… ever? Because they'd shared a few intimate conversations, and he found himself telling her things—personal things—that he'd never spoken of before?

That didn't mean he "cared" about her—which he damned well knew was lass-talk for love. He liked her, of course—and wanted to swive her something fierce—but he was hardly the type to fall in love after a few days. The idea was laughable—ludicrous really. He was much too practical and clearheaded for romantic drivel like "love at first sight." He didn't have a romantic bone in his body. He knew the ladies at court thought him romantic because he espoused the gallantry and courtly gestures of a knight, but that was what was expected. It was all part of the dance. He didn't really believe any of it.

Izzie would probably say it was a performance—another act. Even if it was, so what? The ladies liked it, and there was no harm. It was what was expected of him as one of Bruce's greatest knights.

But he wanted to be *the* greatest and having Elizabeth Douglas by his side would help him achieve that... wouldn't it? Of course it would. She was his perfect complement and would be an asset to him at court. Izzie, on the other hand, didn't even seem to like court that much; she would probably just make him laugh all the time by whispering wry observations in his ear while he was trying to be serious. Elizabeth was rich, landed, connected—all things Izzie was as well, he couldn't help thinking—*and* the most beautiful woman at court. At least that's what people said—and what he'd thought. But that was before he'd noticed Izzie's delicate, timeless, more modest beauty, which was much more...

Ah hell. He had to stop this. He wasn't going to fall in love with anyone. It was a distraction he didn't need. Just because he couldn't forget how she'd looked at him yesterday—all hurt and imploring—and how it had felt as if a boulder was on his chest, didn't mean he should do something rash. He'd given his word, damn it. And for the past six years since he'd returned to the Scottish fold, that had meant something. He wasn't going to do anything to jeopardize what he'd achieved because he was a little confused, and some irritating lass who thought she could see things he couldn't had him all twisted up in knots.

He sure as hell wasn't looking for a way to get out of it.

That wasn't why he was here. He'd entered the abbey rectory and now stood in the private chamber used by the abbot (and the king while he was in the city) waiting—pacing, what the hell was the difference?—while one of the monks fetched Douglas. He'd only sought him out because of what Izzie had hinted at. Aye, it was for Elizabeth's sake that he was here. She wanted this marriage just as much as he did, didn't she? She'd seemed amenable enough when they'd discussed the matter. Perhaps a bit subdued, but he thought that she was just being modest and reserved. He'd never heard her name linked with another man's and she certainly hadn't singled out any men for her attention that he'd noticed.

He'd seen her looking at MacGowan a few times, but he knew that wasn't anything. MacGowan was a childhood friend from her village, but the blacksmith's son was hardly suitable as a prospective suitor.

He turned at the sound of the door opening as his friend and rival strode into the room.

Douglas gave him the black scowl that had helped earn him his epithet and came to a stop, squaring off in front of him as if preparing for a fight. It was an odd tact to take—even for the always-confrontational Douglas—and made Randolph's eyes narrow. Was Douglas anticipating some last-minute objections?

"What's this about, Randy? I thought today was the big day. Isn't it my sister you should be asking to see?"

Randolph ignored the diminutive, which he had Hawk to thank for (he was irritating, too), and answered. "I will, but I wanted to speak to you first."

"I thought we discussed everything yesterday. We've agreed on the tocher, and if you are trying to get more land out of me—"

"It's not that."

His friend's face darkened. Randolph thought he muttered a curse. "Is it Elizabeth? Has she said something?"

Douglas was a little too anxious. Randolph's eyes narrowed suspiciously. "About what?"

"Nothing," Douglas said hastily. Either Randolph's ignorance as to what he might be talking about, or his own realization that he'd given away too much seemed to relax him. Angry and confrontational gave way to gregarious and smiling. "I thought you'd spoken to her and made your intentions clear."

"Aye, but I just wanted to make sure that the lass is not being pressured." They both knew by whom. "I want to make sure that this is what she wants."

"Of course it is."

"She has told you as much?"

"I spoke with her on the very subject last night."

"So there isn't a reason to think she would be… uh, unhappy?" He'd been about to say miserable.

It was Douglas's turn to narrow his eyes suspiciously. "What's this about, Randolph? Where is this coming from? You aren't having second thoughts and trying to get out of it, are you? The contracts have already been drawn up. You gave me your word."

Randolph stiffened. "I know, and I'm not."

"Good," Douglas said with a hard slap on his back. "Then hadn't you better send for my sister?"

That's exactly what he should do. He'd given his word. But for one moment, Randolph felt paralyzed with something akin to panic.

THE STAY OF THE EXECUTIONER'S axe would not be coming from Elizabeth. Izzie could tell from her cousin's distress when she'd returned from her "errand" last night that she would not be the one to put a stop to the betrothal. Indeed, after a talk with her brother, Elizabeth seemed to be resolved to going forward with it. Joanna was obviously furious with her husband for interfering and tried to broach the subject a few times with Elizabeth—"You do not need to rush…"—but her cousin made it clear she did not wish to talk about it. It was all but decided.

From the way Elizabeth jumped every time the door to Joanna's solar opened and closed, Izzie guessed the "but" would be imminent. Thus, it was a surprise when the knock came that the call was for Izzie and not Elizabeth. Walter wished to see her to discuss something "important."

If her heart was pounding a little fast as she hurried across the yard to the abbot's house—which had largely been taken over by the king—she told herself not to be foolish. Walter might wish to see her for any number of reasons. It probably didn't have anything to do with Randolph. But the tiniest part of her wondered if it could. Had she somehow gotten through to him?

She paused when she reached the entry. Walter's squire hadn't said where he'd be waiting. She took a few steps toward the small outer vestibule, which she knew was being used as a receiving chamber for the king, not wanting to disturb anyone. The room was empty, but a few moments later, the door leading to the king's chamber opened and her tall, gangly cousin strode out.

A little younger than herself, the Sixth High Steward of Scotland still looked more youth than man. Freckled, with brown hair tinged with a great deal of red, Walter had the ruddy good looks that would grow more pronounced with age. His seemingly perpetual good cheer and broad smile brought a twinkle to his blue eyes that never ceased to make her smile in return.

"That was fast, cousin. I'm sorry not to be here when you arrived. I hope you were not waiting long?"

Embarrassed by her obvious eagerness, Izzie tried not to flush—unsuccessfully. "Your squire said I should come right away."

"Aye," Walter said with another smile. "I have some good news."

"You do?"

"I've had a request for your hand that I have been led to believe will be agreeable to you."

Surprise—shock—stole her breath. Her already pounding heart started to hammer with anticipation as the realization surged through her in a giddy wave. She knew it wasn't just her! Randolph had seen what she had and changed his mind. He'd chosen her.

"I am," she said, unable to contain the eagerness in her voice.

The enthusiasm of her reaction seemed to take Walter aback. "I'm thrilled to hear that, Izzie. It's a fine match—an excellent one. Your brother can't speak highly enough of him. He said in his missive that you'd gotten to know one another recently and seemed to enjoy one another's company." Missive? Izzie's heart plummeted before her head caught up. "I know he's a bit older than you and has been married before, but maturity and patience can be great benefits in a bridegroom, I've been told."

His face reddened, and she would have wondered what he'd been told if her heart wasn't shattering all over the floor.

Not Randolph then. Had she really thought it might be? She felt… God, she felt like such a fool.

"With the lands in your tocher abutting his, you will have the largest baronies in Berwickshire."

"Sir William de Vipont," she said, understanding. "The Lord of Langton has asked for my hand."

"Did you think it was someone else?" Walter asked with more perceptiveness than she would have wished. "If there is someone else who interests you, I can—"

"Nay," Izzie cut him off, barely hiding her horror at the idea of him finding out the truth. Her foolishness was bad enough without anyone else discovering the level of her stupidity. "There is no one."

Walter beamed. "Good. Shall I write him back and tell him you accept?"

She had no reason not to. It was indeed a good match. Sir William was a highly respected baron of vast lands in the Borders. He had been closely aligned to the Earl of March—and thus the English—until about a year ago. But Izzie's eldest brother, Alexander, had fought with Sir William when he'd made his peace with Bruce and had come to look at him as something of a mentor.

The last time Alexander had been home—before the most recent time with Sir Stephen, that is—he'd introduced them. She'd liked the older warrior, who was probably in his midthirties, very much. He had the refined manners that came from spending so many years in England with the sturdy, no-nonsense battle-hard look of a Scot.

Her heart had immediately gone out to him when he'd spoken of the loss of his young wife the year before in childbirth. A son who hadn't survived. The unapologetic emotion in his voice had moved her greatly.

It hadn't been difficult to guess what her brother was hoping for, and she might have been amendable to the idea had Sir Stephen not arrived in the interim and swept her off her feet.

And now there was Randolph. Or was there? Was it all in her head?

Seeing her hesitate, Walter added, "He can protect you, Izzie."

From Sir Stephen and men of his ilk. Walter didn't need to say it; she understood. And she didn't doubt it. Sir William was the kind of man built to make women feel safe. Formidable in size and strength, he would hold fast to what was his with a ferocity that few men would dare challenge.

She nodded. "I know. It is an excellent offer, and one I'm sure I would be hard-pressed to refuse."

"But," Walter said with a frown, anticipating her next word. "You are refusing him?"

Izzie shook her head. Her heart wanted to, but her heart had already been proven a fool once—maybe twice. She didn't know why she was hesitating, but she couldn't believe she'd been so wrong. "Nay, I would just ask for a few days to consider it."

Walter grinned, obviously relieved. "Of course. Take all the time you need. I know lasses do not to like to appear too eager. It won't hurt to keep him guessing for a few days," he added with a wink.

She wished she could return it, but it was taking all her

effort to hold back the tears that suddenly seemed to be prickling behind her eyes. Instead she nodded.

"It's better to let the excitement die down anyway. You don't want your news to get lost."

Izzie paused, everything inside her having suddenly grown very still and very cold. "What excitement?"

"I've just heard from Jamie that Randolph is asking Ella to marry him. The king has ordered a feast for the midday meal today with an even bigger one tomorrow after the betrothal ceremony."

The blood slid from her face, and her eyes widened with shock. "The what?"

Walter laughed at her reaction, not seeing the pain that had provoked it. "Aye, I know it's fast, but Jamie doesn't want to waste any time with the English preparing to march in a few months. With everyone of import already here, he said there was no reason to wait." Walter leaned down. "Between us, I think they are planning something with the castle. Knowing Randolph, it will be dramatic."

But Izzie wasn't listening. All she could think of was that it couldn't be true.

CHAPTER EIGHT

IT *WAS* TRUE. HE'D DONE it. Izzie couldn't believe it. But not long after she returned to the guesthouse after meeting with Walter, Elizabeth came bursting into the room with a smile so exaggerated and forced it seemed in danger of shattering like a piece of overblown glass.

She and Randolph were to marry, she said. She was "thrilled" (which didn't explain why her eyes were sparkling with tears) and hoped they would be happy for her. Izzie managed a long hug (mostly so her cousin wouldn't see the tears in her own eyes), but Joanna was so disappointed, she could barely murmur a choked, emotion-filled congratulations. There would be a feast to celebrate at the midday meal, Elizabeth continued with enough brightness to light the city at night, an even bigger celebration tomorrow after the betrothal ceremony, and a wedding to plan for in three weeks.

Three weeks?

Izzie's knees buckled. She felt as though she'd been kicked in the stomach. She hoped no one had seen her stagger.

"Is something wrong, Izzie?" Elizabeth asked. Izzie cursed, realizing her cousin *had* been watching her. "You look a little pale."

"I'm not feeling very well," Izzie answered truthfully.

She felt ill. She must have looked it, too. Both Elizabeth and Joanna became immediately concerned.

"Perhaps you should go lie down for a while," Joanna

suggested. The sympathy in Jamie's wife's gaze made Izzie wonder if the other woman suspected something of the truth. "Elizabeth and I will discuss all the details and fill you in on everything when you feel better." *Or never,* Joanna seemed to add silently.

Izzie nodded gratefully.

Elizabeth looked so worried, Izzie almost felt guilty for misleading her as to the source of her illness. "I do hope you aren't coming down with something serious. I don't want you to miss the ceremony tomorrow. I need you there."

Izzie's stomach lurched at the thought; she feared her paleness had turned a little green. "Me, too," she said with halfheartedness that she hoped her cousin would attribute to her illness.

An illness that, as it turned out, did last through the betrothal ceremony.

Elizabeth pretended to understand, but Izzie knew her cousin was hurt by her absence. Izzie wanted to be there for her—truly she did—but she just couldn't do it. Maybe she was a coward, maybe she was selfish, maybe she wasn't ready to accept the truth and wanted to delude herself a little longer, she didn't know. But she couldn't stand witness to Randolph binding himself to her cousin and pretend it didn't matter. Pretend it didn't hurt. Pretend that she didn't want him for herself.

So she stayed away, tending her wounds in private, while her cousin tried to convince them that she hadn't made the biggest mistake of her life. Izzie and Joanna weren't fooled; the only question was how long Elizabeth could continue to fool herself.

The day after the betrothal ceremony, Izzie had "recovered" enough to join her cousin and Joanna on a prewedding shopping trip up and down the high street of Edinburgh.

She even managed to enjoy herself and feel no more than a tiny prick of jealousy when Elizabeth started picking out fabrics for her wedding gown. Izzie was back to her wry, good-natured, lighthearted self and firmly back in her supportive cousin position.

She'd made too much of it, Izzie told herself. She'd been swept up by passion and confused into thinking it might be something more. Randolph was a real-life hero, for goodness' sake. What woman wouldn't be a little overcome by his attentions?

She was like Annie. He'd made a woman who didn't think she'd ever have a faerie tale feel like a princess for a few days, but it hadn't been real. And it certainly wasn't anything to build a future on. Even if they had more in common than she realized, even if he'd surprised her that day at the pond with his kindness and playfulness, even if he wasn't as unfeeling as she'd thought, and even if there was more to him than the "perfect" knight, he still wasn't for her.

She didn't want to live her life on stage as the wife of a legend in the making. She didn't want to always have to dress perfectly, with no hairs out of place, and be worried about what she said. She liked the quiet of the countryside and the calm of hearth and home. She liked to read before the fire and sit by candlelight dreaming up ways of improving the castle. She liked to make wry observations from tables below the salt, not sit at the high table and have to glitter and entertain.

She had almost succeeded in convincing herself it was for the best. But then, two days after the betrothal and four since Izzie had last seen Randolph (not that she was counting), Elizabeth came bursting into her room in tears and told her what Randolph and Thom MacGowan intended to do.

It changed everything.

AFTER THE MEETING WITH DOUGLAS on Monday morning, Randolph had kept his word and sent for Elizabeth. When he stumbled awkwardly through the proposal (he was glad he didn't need to feign romance with Elizabeth because his mind had gone blank with anything lighthearted and charming to say), and managed an only slightly less awkward kiss that evening, which was possibly the most chaste one he'd ever given and felt like he was kissing his sister (thankfully he'd managed not to shudder), he told himself it wasn't anything to worry about. It was just the lingering irritation toward Izzie.

Aye, he knew *exactly* who he had to blame for the way his heart started to race at the oddest times, how his mind felt as if some of Sutherland's black powder had gone off inside, why he broke out into a cold sweat when he'd said his vows, and the way his stomach seemed to be constantly twisted in knots.

He was furious with her for putting him in this position. She'd made him feel as if he was doing something wrong— as if he'd made some kind of *mistake*. But Izzie expected too much, damn it. What else could he have done?

She would see; it would be better for her this way. It would only hurt her more when he couldn't give her what she wanted.

He would tell her exactly that, but… Where the hell was she?

He finally had asked Elizabeth while they were seated at the dais for the betrothal celebration feast.

Sick? Was she all right? He hoped Elizabeth hadn't noticed that he'd nearly jumped up from the bench when she'd told him.

If she did, she didn't comment. But she seemed to sense his concern; she put her hand on his arm with a smile. "I do not think it is anything serious. But it is kind of you to ask. I know you and Izzie didn't get off to the best start, but I hope that you will be friends. She is very dear to me, and I think once you get to know her, you will like her. I'm hoping she will come stay with us for a while after we are married." Good thing she wasn't looking at him so she didn't see him blanch. *Good God! Not a chance in Hades.* "She is very smart and witty. Even at a very dark time in my life she could always make me laugh and see the ridiculous in things."

Randolph didn't say anything; he didn't need to. He understood well enough. The lass had managed to make him smile while shoveling shi—dung, hadn't she? Not to mention pushing him into a damned pond. He forced his mind away before he started remembering what else had happened at that pond.

Damn. He adjusted his braies. Too late.

This was crazy, damn it. He shouldn't be thinking about her. He was going to marry her cousin.

Randolph tugged at the neck of his surcoat, having that can't breathe feeling again. A cold sweat broke out across his forehead and his heart started to race. He grabbed his goblet and took a long drink of wine. He hadn't made a mistake, damn it. And even if he had—which he hadn't—it was too late to do anything about it.

Fortunately, Randolph didn't have long to dwell on it. His attention was diverted elsewhere. On Wednesday, the day after the betrothal ceremony, the king had called him in for a special council meeting. It seemed that MacGowan had figured out a way to implement Randolph's idea to climb Castle Rock after all. He'd somehow got the idea to modify a few steel spikes that he would hammer into the rock and use to span the twenty-five foot stretch of sheer cliff face that had made climbing the cliff impossible.

At least it *had* been impossible—until now. Randolph knew that if MacGowan could pull this off and lead him up the rocky cliff to take the castle, it would be the kind of miraculous feat that would equal, if not surpass, Douglas's recent taking of Roxburgh and ensure Randolph's place in history. His name would be uttered in the hallowed echelons of other great military heroes, men renowned as great tacticians. English leaders such as Richard the Lionheart, William Marshal, and their old enemy Edward Longshanks; and Scotsmen like William Wallace, Sir Andrew Murray, James Douglas—blast it—and Robert the Bruce.

The king agreed to let them try, and the plan was set in motion. On Thursday night (or Friday morning, depending on how you looked at it), Bruce and a group of men would stage a diversionary attack at the south gate of the castle to draw the garrison away from the wall, while Randolph led a small group of climbers up after MacGowan to scale the north face of Castle Rock and surprise the soldiers defending the gate from behind.

No one overestimated their chances. Even with MacGowan's spikes, they didn't have much of one. The climb could fail.

Or worse.

That they could die, Randolph understood, but with military immortality on the line (not to mention putting an end to the cursed siege), the risk was worth it.

At least that's what he thought until he *did* nearly die.

When the night in question came around, miraculously MacGowan's spikes had held. After hammering them into cracks in the rock at three-foot intervals, the skilled climber had been able to make it past the twenty-five-foot span of sheer cliff side to a plateau near the base of the castle's rock wall. From there, he'd tossed down a rope ladder fitted with wooden boards to the rest of the men waiting below. Randolph was the first man up the ladder. He'd been about halfway up when disaster—or near disaster—struck. A soldier on patrol from the castle above tossed a stone over the wall. Whether it was because he thought he'd heard something or because he was just bored, they would never know. But the stone found a target—him. It struck Randolph in the helm with enough force to make him see black for a moment—a very important moment, as he'd been in the process of climbing and lost his footing and hold on the rope ladder. He fell backward and would have fallen to his death if MacGowan hadn't dove off the side of the cliff toward him and managed to get a few fingers on the neck of his leather *cotun*. The blacksmith's son-turned-warrior and soon-to-be latest member of the Highland Guard had saved Randolph's life.

It had happened so fast Randolph hadn't had time to panic. He had, however, had time to see someone's face.

Why he should think of Izzie as he was about to fall to his death, he didn't know.

But he suspected, damn it. And he wasn't happy about it. The lass had obviously bewitched him.

Even now, as he celebrated what was the greatest accomplishment of his life so far—the ploy at the gate had worked and they had indeed taken the castle—he couldn't stop looking at her.

She looked a little pale. Was she still not feeling well? His heart raced. What the hell was the matter with her?

And why hadn't she looked at him? She was seated at a trestle table with Joanna Douglas only a few feet away, but not once had her eyes strayed to his position on the dais. Shouldn't she at least offer her congratulations? God knows the lass wasn't easily impressed, but surely *this* warranted something. He'd taken a castle that no one thought could be taken and almost died in the taking. Didn't she care?

Their eyes met for the first time in five days, and he felt the shock of it like a bolt of lightning down his spine. It wasn't a pleasant experience. It hurt. A lot.

Aye, she did care. That was the problem. A big one, as it turned out, because so did he. More than he wanted to.

His chest was still burning when she turned away. He did the same, returning his attention to the celebration. This was the happiest day of his life. He was going to bloody well enjoy it.

With the help of quite a bit of wine, he did. Mostly. But when some of the men left to begin slighting some of the castle walls, Randolph didn't mind leaving to supervise.

He glanced once more at Izzie, but her head was again fixed in the opposite direction.

He was about to stand up and make his excuses when Elizabeth stopped him. She'd been oddly distracted throughout the meal, which he hadn't thought too much about as it enabled him not to worry about her picking up on his own distraction.

"My lord, might we speak in private for a moment."

I can't marry you. Randolph paled in horror. Christ, for a moment he thought he'd said the words aloud. Whatever he was thinking, it was too late. *Too late,* damn it.

He forced a smile to his face. "I should like nothing more, but might it wait?" Presumably until he pulled his head out of his arse and trusted himself enough not to do or say anything stupid. "My uncle has put me in charge of the destruction of the castle, and the men are waiting for me."

"Of course."

He almost changed his mind when he saw her disappointment. Something clearly was bothering her. But it probably had to do with the wedding, and frankly that was a subject he just couldn't discuss right now. She would see right through his lack of enthusiasm.

After thanking her for her understanding, Randolph left to join his men. But he wasn't just going to supervise. He was looking forward to wielding a hammer to take down the blasted wall himself. Anything to take his mind off thinking that he'd made a mistake.

THE LAST TWENTY-FOUR HOURS had alternated between the darkest most miserable lows and the brightest most joyous highs. The realization of what the men intended to do brought all their secrets to light. The thought of Thom MacGowan dying had forced Elizabeth to admit that she'd been lying to herself—she could not go through with the betrothal no matter how horrible the scandal. Izzie, too, upon learning that Randolph intended to join MacGowan on his suicide mission, betrayed her horror and, in turn, her feelings.

The harrowing, gut-wrenching hours while the women waited for news from the castle were not some Izzie cared to repeat—ever. When the bell from the castle rang out in the middle of the night, and they realized the men had done it, she'd cried tears of relief and happiness and celebrated along with everyone else.

But even knowing that Elizabeth intended to break the

engagement didn't make the celebration feast any easier. For days Izzie had been blaming the betrothal and Randolph's refusal to break his word for keeping them apart, but what if that wasn't it? What if even with the impediment between them removed, he still wouldn't admit his feelings for her?

Izzie was painfully conscious that the reprieve from the betrothal had come from Ella. Randolph hadn't chosen her.

The thought was sobering and heart twisting. And watching him didn't make it any better. Randolph always had that aura of hero around him, but now it was worse. Now he wasn't just a hero, he'd become a legend. She watched him glitter like a star beside her cousin and the king from the corner of her eye. Watched the women fawning over him—even with Elizabeth sitting right there!

How could Izzie fit into that world?

She didn't. But the one time their gazes had caught gave her hope. She'd seen something there. *Felt* something even from her position below the dais. He did care about her. She knew it.

So when her cousin left to find Thom MacGowan, Izzie volunteered to take her cousin's note and find Randolph to explain that her cousin was breaking the betrothal.

Though the midday feast had ended hours ago, the air of celebration still hung about the city as she made her way up the mile-long high street that separated Holyrood Abbey from the castle with her escort. Joanna's brother Richard had offered to walk with her as he was heading up to the castle himself. The king and most of his men had removed to the castle, but the ladies—and their husbands in the case of Jamie—would stay in the abbey for now.

Even if she no longer needed to worry about Sir Stephen, Izzie was grateful for Richard's presence as men—drunken soldiers mostly—spilled out of alehouses on more than one occasion. Richard proved to be a good roadblock, as he put himself between her and the path of more than one staggering drunk.

It was nearing twilight, and with the fading light, Izzie

was grateful for the fur-lined cloak that she'd donned as the mild almost-spring day gave way to the cold winter hours of night. By the time they'd reached the castle, the sun was a delicate wisp of pinkish orange on the horizon. With all the thick, dark gray stone walls, it seemed even colder.

It was hard to believe that less than twenty-four hours ago this castle was filled with a garrison of Englishmen. Elizabeth had told her that those who had not died in the fighting had already been sent back to England after vowing not to return. Her cousin had also mentioned that Randolph had been put in charge of supervising the destruction of the castle walls, which was why she was here and not at the siege camp.

She and Richard were still laughing about the last drunk who'd mistaken Richard for his wife and tried to kiss him, as they strode through the gate.

There were a number of people milling about the courtyard—soldiers and villagers who seemed reluctant to leave the celebration. She stood on her tiptoes and pretended to look around. "Should we find the barber?" she teased with a playful tug on one of Richard's shoulder-length blond locks. "Perhaps it's time for a trim?"

The young warrior shook his head with disgust. "If he mistook me for his wife, perhaps we should give her a sword."

Izzie laughed again. He was right. Richard was at least a few inches over six feet and although young, already thick with the imposing muscle typical of his Norse forbearers. The woman would have to be formidable indeed to be confused with him.

"Besides," he added with a wink. "The lasses like my hair long."

Izzie couldn't help smiling as she shook her head. He was incorrigible and a horrible flirt, but she'd grown fond of both Joanna's brothers. "I'm sure they do. And which poor unsuspecting lass is to have her heart broken tonight?"

"You can save them all if you just say the word." He took her hand and clasped it to his chest. "Put me out of my misery, dearest Isabel, and run away with me."

She laughed again and gave him a hard shove. "Go spin your silken tongue to someone who doesn't know you so well. But you should have care, one of these days I may take you up on one of your proposals just to teach you a lesson."

He grinned unrepentantly. "And why do I think you actually could?"

Isabel would have given him another shove and told him to get if a dark shadow hadn't fallen across them both.

"What the Devil is going on here?"

She looked up onto the familiar darkened features. It appeared she didn't need to find Randolph; he'd found her.

CHAPTER NINE

NOT FIVE MINUTES AFTER LEAVING the relaxing, steam-filled kitchen where his sore muscles had found relief in the hot water of a wooden tub, those same muscles were tight and knotted again.

At first Randolph thought he'd imagined her. He'd been thinking about Izzie—and what in Hades he was going to do about Elizabeth—when he'd caught a glimpse of the laughing couple as he left the kitchen on his way to the Great Hall. That was when he'd known he wasn't imagining her because he sure as hell wouldn't be imagining Izzie with a big Viking. It was only as he drew closer—stormed across the yard, actually—that he realized the Viking was Douglas's young brother-in-law, which didn't necessarily improve his temper any. The lad already had something of a reputation around camp for his prowess both on and off the battlefield.

Christ, Randolph was considering breaking his word for her—she was right, he'd proved himself many times over, and even if he hadn't before, the taking of Edinburgh Castle should have put his past to rest for good—and she was flirting and carrying on with the lad as if she had no care in the world?

Wasn't she supposed to care about *him*? Well, it certainly wasn't looking like it. And unless he'd been mistaken, the lad had just propositioned her, and she hadn't exactly discouraged him.

"My lord," the lad said with a bow of his head.

"Sir Thomas," Izzie said at the same time, not with a bow but with a small frown wrinkling her nose.

It might have been cute if he wasn't so irritated. Had his interruption annoyed her? Too bloody bad! His hands fisted at his side.

"What are you doing here?" he demanded.

It certainly wasn't his most gallant moment. But she just lifted that perfectly arched brow of hers in a way that only added to that burr under the plaid feeling. If she rolled her eyes or started to laugh, he wasn't going to be responsible for what happened next.

"Looking for you, actually." She turned to the lad and gave him a brilliant smile, which only made Randolph's fists squeeze harder. She'd never smiled at him like that, damn it. "Thanks for accompanying me, Richard. I will have one of the earl's men see me back."

Izzie might not have any idea of the kind of torment she was giving Randolph, but the lad—Richard—apparently did. He looked at Randolph, frowned, and then looked back to her. "Are you sure? I don't mind sticking around awhile in case you need me."

Insolent pup! Randolph made a sound suspiciously like a growl and took a step forward. The two men were of size, but Randolph had years of experience on him—they both knew there would be no contest.

"She won't," Randolph snapped with a sharp edge to his voice that could not be mistaken for anything other than a threat.

He had to give the lad credit. Richard was intimidated, but he still turned back to confirm with Izzie. She frowned chastisingly at Randolph, clearly not understanding why he was being so rude and foul-tempered.

"I'll be fine." She smiled. "Say hello to our friend if you run into him on your way back down the hill."

The lad made a face. "If he does that again, I'll find that barber myself."

She laughed, and Richard was lucky he moved off. Instead Randolph took his fury out on the fair-haired tormentor before him. "What the hell was that about?"

She crossed her arms impatiently, and he swore he could almost hear the sound of a toe tapping. "It's a private jest." He didn't like the sound of that at all and would have told her so, but she didn't give him a chance. "Whatever is the matter with you? You were quite rude to Richard, and he was doing me a favor."

"I'm sure he was," he said snidely.

She drew her chin up and looked down her nose at him as if she were the Queen of bloody England. "What is that supposed to mean?"

"It means you'll be careful if you have care for your reputation—the lad is known for having his way with the lasses."

She stared—gaped really—at him, clearly dumbfounded. "Surely, you jest? This coming from the biggest rogue in Scotland?"

He bristled. "It's not the same."

She laughed—actually it was more of a scoff. "It's exactly the same. But don't worry, my lord, not all of us are worried about our reputations."

Was she referring to his or hers? Although he wasn't sure either was preferable. He grabbed her arm and hauled her against him. How did she do this? A few minutes in her presence, and he was losing his mind. "What the Devil do you mean by that?"

Very slowly, she unwrapped his fingers from around her arm. "Whatever you wish it to mean. What is wrong with you? You certainly aren't acting like a man who just performed one of the greatest military feats in history."

"I didn't think you noticed."

He was aware that he sounded more than a little petulant. But damn it, what did it take to impress her?

She looked into his eyes. "I noticed," she said quietly. "I have never been so terrified in my life." She paused, and the emotion in her gaze made something in his chest shift. "You could have died."

And just like that, the jealousy—for even he realized

that's what it was—unwound its tight grip on his muscles and fled. He was an idiot. She cared for him, how could he have doubted it?

"I might have," he admitted ruefully, "were it not for MacGowan."

She'd obviously heard what had happened because she did not ask what he meant.

"That is what I wish to speak with you about," she said. He frowned again. MacGowan? "Is there someplace private we can talk?"

He wasn't sure that was a good idea. He was already noticing how good she smelled and how velvety soft her skin looked. The lass had the most beautiful skin—it looked unreal. It had felt unreal also. He shook off the memory, which was already leading to a rush of blood in uncomfortable places. "What about?"

"I'd prefer to discuss it with you inside—where we cannot be overheard and where the mist isn't turning my bones to ice."

It was obviously important and personal. The Great Hall was crowded with people who'd decided to blend the midday meal with the evening meal with celebrating, and his uncle was using the private solar behind it. There were a few storerooms they might use, but he led her to a nearby guard tower that he knew was presently unoccupied. He could control himself for a few minutes.

He grabbed a torch as he went inside and used it to light the coals in the brazier that he found in what presumably had been the captain's lodgings. Ignoring the box bed along one side of the room, he pulled up a stool for her to sit on, but she shook her head.

She looked uncomfortable and maybe a little nervous.

He frowned. "What is this about, Izzie?"

He couldn't help but notice how pretty she looked tonight. Her cheeks were rosy from the cold and her lips were so red it looked as if she'd been biting them.

Christ, not the thing he should be thinking about. Being here like this was dangerous. God, how he wanted her.

What a mess. What the hell was he going to do?

She fished around in the leather purse that she wore tied to her waist and pulled out what appeared to be a folded piece of parchment. "It's about your betrothal—or rather your former betrothal. I hope you will not be too distressed to hear that my cousin realized she is in love with someone else and can no longer marry you." He was too shocked to react; he simply stared at her. This only seemed to make her more jittery. Her hands fluttered as she handed him the note. "Here. She wrote you a note to apologize."

He took the note, quickly scanned it, and slowly crumpled it in his hand. He could feel the anger rising inside him, mixing with the unfamiliar taste of humiliation. "And she thought a quick note of apology would suffice to break a betrothal that has been negotiated for months between two of the most important families in Scotland?"

His voice was deceptively calm as the storm of emotion unleashed inside him. The piece of parchment in his fist had become a tight ball. He threw it into the fire of the brazier where it quickly caught flame and disintegrated into black.

IZZIE WAS HAVING SECOND THOUGHTS about the wisdom of her being the one to break the news to him. Too late she remembered that the messenger was sometimes killed.

She'd known he would be angry, but she'd thought that he would also be... what? Relieved? Happy because he could marry her? Aye, maybe both those things, foolish though they were.

Realizing it was too late to back out now, she stood her ground and told herself to be patient. It was the shock. "Ella wanted to speak to you in person. She said she tried at the feast."

"And tonight?"

Heat rose to her cheeks. "She had something else to do." Elizabeth had gone to see Thom MacGowan. She intended to force him to listen to her, and Izzie was fairly sure how she intended to do that. "I told her I would tell you."

"Which I'm sure you were happy to do," he said caustically. "No doubt this is exactly what you wanted. Did you tell her something? Is that it?"

What *you* wanted, he'd said. Not him.

The heat in her cheeks grew hotter. Did he think her that desperate to run to her cousin when he wouldn't put a stop to it? She looked down—well up—at him with not a small amount of rebuke. "If you are referring to what has happened between us, I didn't say a word before Ella made her decision. As I said, my cousin is in love with someone else. I tried to warn you, but you didn't want to see it."

All of a sudden he did see it. His face drained. "MacGowan? God's blood, could this be any worse? Is that who she thinks she is in love with?" He uttered a very crude curse. "She has broken a betrothal to me to run off with a blacksmith's son? She has made laughingstocks of us both." He took her arm. "Tell me you are jesting. God, please, tell me this is a joke."

Izzie told herself not to overreact—he was speaking out of anger—but was his image the only thing he was thinking about?

What about me?

"It is not a joke," she replied. "Ella loves him—she has for a long time, although she only realized it recently. There will be talk, but she is strong enough to weather it." He was, too. "It is your pride speaking right now," she said. "I know you don't love her."

"What the hell does that have to do with it? She has brought humiliation and dishonor down upon us both." He cringed. "God, I can just hear it now."

Izzie stared at him. She knew it was her own disappointment at her unrealistic expectations of what his reaction would be at work, but she wasn't sure she liked him very much right now. The arrogant, self-important knight who took himself too seriously and was cold beneath a layer of surface charm had returned.

Maybe he had never left. But then why did it feel as if

her heart were breaking?

"I am sorry you are disappointed," she said quietly. "I will leave you now. I'm sure my cousin and Jamie can answer any other questions you might have."

THROUGH THE HAZE OF ANGER Randolph caught something in her voice—something was wrong. Very wrong.

Ah hell. What was he doing? He shouldn't be lashing out at her. None of this was Izzie's fault.

"Wait," he said, grabbing her wrist. "I'm sorry. Your cousin deserves my anger—not you."

"I hoped she might deserve something else. Something like your gratitude."

It took him a moment to realize what she meant. "My God, you are right." He didn't have to break his word to have Izzie. "It is not a complete disaster. When we marry, it won't be so bad."

He thought she'd be happy, but for some reason she looked like he'd just kicked her. "So I am the consolation? The way to improve your image? By marrying me, people will think *you* wanted out of it so it won't look as if the great Sir Thomas Randolph has been thrown over for a blacksmith's son, is that it?"

Randolph was completely taken aback. What was she talking about? She wasn't a consolation. He *did* want to marry her. Now he would be able to. "Of course not. That isn't it at all."

"Then why do you want to marry me?"

Randolph felt those hackles rising again. Bloody hell, why did she always have to push him into making some kind of declaration he didn't want to make. He told her he had no intention of falling in love. Couldn't she just be happy and leave it at that? Although she didn't look happy at all right now; she looked as if he'd stepped on her puppy. He tugged at his surcoat again, feeling that uncomfortable pressure in his chest that cut off his breath. "You know why.

I want you."

"And fidelity? Is that a vow you intend to keep or will that interfere with your reputation? The perfect knight who everyone loves, but who loves no one."

Randolph didn't like the way this conversation was going at all. The anger that had disappeared on the realization that he could marry her was back full force. She was being unreasonable—unrealistic—trying to pin him down. The fact that he hadn't so much as looked at another woman since she arrived didn't mean he was a horse to be led around by the bit. He wasn't like those poor sod friends of his that had allowed themselves to be trapped with one woman forever. He was sure he would shudder at the thought later.

But he sure as hell wasn't going to make any promises he couldn't keep, so instead he said nothing. Maybe that was answer enough.

"I didn't think so." She pulled her wrist away from his hold. "I thank you for the offer, my lord—assuming that was a proposal—but I'm afraid I must decline."

Randolph swore, realizing his second proposal had been even worse than the first. He told himself she didn't mean it. She was upset and had every right to be. But how she managed to turn him into someone who was about as gallant and charming as Ewen Lamont—the tracker of the Highland Guard was well known for his blunt manner and lack of social niceties—he didn't know. Somehow he seemed to always say the wrong thing with her; he didn't have the words to adequately convey what he felt.

"Damn it, I'm sorry," he said, raking his fingers back through his still-damp hair. "I bungled that pretty egregiously, didn't I? But you caught me off guard."

"Aye," she said. "I suppose I did. But I think that might have been a good thing. I see things clearly now."

He frowned, not liking the sound of that. "What do you mean?"

She straightened her spine and pushed up her chin. He might have thought her indifferent had he not seen it quivering. "I mean we would not suit."

He didn't like how she was trying to move away from him so he brought her closer. Aye, that felt better; now he could relax. "I think we would suit quite well."

"You mean in bed?"

Christ, the things she said. Of course he meant in bed, but there were other things as well. "That is more than most husbands and wives can say, but we also share similar interests. I did promise to write you a chanson, didn't I?" The reference to the wart and moles didn't get the barest twitch of a smile. "And you did say that you wanted to come see the drawings I have of the changes I'd like to make to some of my castles," he added teasingly.

But clearly she wasn't in the mood to laugh or remember his warning about men and drawings—or of the interests they shared.

"That isn't enough for me."

It was simply stated, which somehow made it worse. He hated when she was like this. Too self-possessed. Too confident. Too bloody sure of herself. Why it was almost as if she didn't need him! As if she could walk away and never look back. The thought made his heart pound fast again. "Damn it, Izzie. What more do you want from me?"

He wasn't the only one getting angry. Her icy demeanor cracked a little to reveal some of the hurt and anger simmering underneath. "I want someone who doesn't care what people think and hasn't confused image with substance. Who isn't afraid to make a mistake and doesn't think that greatness means perfection. Someone whose first thought on hearing that he is no longer bound by a betrothal he doesn't want is relief and happiness that he can marry *me*. I want someone who wants my love more than he wants the love of everyone around him. I want someone who will be loyal to me both in and out of the bedchamber because nothing else would ever occur to him. I want someone who would choose me first even if I don't glitter like a diamond or look like a princess from a faerie tale. I have no wish to live in faerie tale, my lord. I want something real—someone real."

Randolph had no idea what she was talking about—she was so beautiful she made his chest hurt every time he looked at her. And as for the other accusations... "Are you sure it isn't you living in the faerie tale? I'm surprised that anyone would meet those requirements."

"You did—or I thought you did—for a while."

There it was, that certainty again. He didn't like it. He didn't like it one bit. She had that obstinate, dig-in-her-heels look on her face that told him he was losing control of the situation.

He probably should have let her go and given her time to think. She would come around on her own. No matter what she said now, he knew she wanted to marry him. She cared about him, and once she realized she could not force him to make declarations or promises, she would change her mind. Perhaps she would even apologize to him for all those unflattering things she'd said about him.

Aye, he definitely liked the thought of that!

But something about her expression stopped him from letting her go. She looked so final—so *resolved*—that he didn't do the prudent thing. He did the very *im*prudent thing and reached for her. He would make her see the truth right now.

CHAPTER TEN

IZZIE DIDN'T THING RANDOLPH BELIEVED her. But when he pulled her into his arms, she wondered if maybe part of him did. If maybe he understood that she was going to walk away, and he'd decided to do whatever it took to stop her.

She should have pushed him away. She would have, were she not desperate to do whatever it took as well. Was "wanting" enough? Was she asking for too much? Would making love make up for not being loved? Could she marry him knowing this would be all he would ever give her?

When his mouth covered hers, she knew she was going to find out. There was something different about his kiss this time. It was still incredible. His lips were still warm and soft and knew exactly how to move against hers to make her knees weak and her insides turn to mush, she could still taste the faint hint of cinnamon, and the body that was pressed against hers was still warm and solid with steely hard muscle, but the edge of control that she hadn't even realized had been there was gone. There was nothing holding him back; the reins had snapped, and the full force of his passion for her had been unleashed.

It was a rather heady feeling, realizing that he was wild for her. And God help her, she was wild for him, too. She prayed it was enough as she was going to gamble her innocence to find out.

Their mouths clashed, their tongues sparred, their bodies pressed together as if they could melt into one, as if any sliver of air that dared to come between them had to be smothered. His hand slid through her hair to grip the back of her head, to bring her mouth more fully against him, and she moaned at the heated sensation of his tongue delving deep inside her. Stroking. Circling. Demanding more and more from her until she couldn't stand another minute. Until she was desperate for his touch and the feel of his body moving against hers.

He seemed to understand her frantic moans and groans and gave her what she wanted. He cupped her bottom with one hand and lifted her hard against him—or rather *he* was hard. Very hard. The feel of his manhood wedged tightly between her legs sent a blast of sensation exploding inside her. She was hot and tingly, every inch of her skin alive and sensitive.

It was a relief when he started to pull off her cloak and push her back toward the bed. But it didn't last long. As soon as she hit the straw of the mattress, it was as if she were fevered and tossing off the covers at night, trying to cool a body that could not be cooled.

The layers of clothing between them seemed so binding and confining that she wasn't surprised when he started to pull them off. She was more surprised that he didn't rip them off.

His cloak and surcoat were tossed to the ground. The sleeveless houppelande that she wore over her gown followed. The wide-necked fitted wool gown underneath was not as easy to remove, but proving his experience with divesting women of their clothing—*don't think of that now*—he magically managed to untie and loosen the laces at her back to slide it down to her waist.

It was then, when her breasts were covered by only the thin linen of her shift, that modesty finally intervened. The protest, however, died in her throat when he straightened from his kneeling position leaning over her on the bed (good lord, how had that happened?) to remove his shirt.

Izzie gasped. It wasn't exactly shock; it was more like admiration that penetrated to her bones—although the markings did surprise her.

She'd known from the solid feel of his body against her that he would be well-formed, but she hadn't anticipated precisely *how* well-formed. Nor, frankly, had she thought that the size of his muscles or the power of his body would matter. In other words, she didn't think herself that silly and superficial to have her head turned by an impressive display of masculinity. But her head was turned all right, and her eyes were fixed on his chest, absorbing every taut line, every sharp delineation, and every powerful bulge.

She might have thought he'd been chipped from stone, but there was no sculptor—even a divine one—who could have created such perfection. Those arms and chest had been forged by hours and hours of wielding a sword on the battlefield. For all his knightly charms, the man was a battle-hard warrior through and through. His shoulders were broad and square, his chest lean and powerful, his arms big and strong, and his stomach ribbed with thick bands of muscle that she had to fight the urge to reach out and run her fingers over.

He had quite a number of scars, which only seemed fitting for this finely honed weapon of war. His skin was smooth and golden, except for the dark, ancient-looking markings on one arm and shoulder that covered him almost like a sleeve. She'd heard of such marks before, but she'd never seen any—and she certainly hadn't expected to see such a primitive design on such a refined knight. But somehow that only added to its base appeal. Beneath the knightly garb, the markings seemed to be telling her that he was *all* Highland warrior.

When she finally managed to lift her eyes from the jaw-dropping display, it was to meet his amused gaze. He must have read her surprise. "It's a long story," he said anticipating the question. "But suffice it to say, I did it to shut a few people up and remind them that I was just as much a Highlander as they were."

"Did it hurt?" she asked, her fingers tracing the lines of the markings.

"Like the bloody Devil," he answered with a grin.

"It's perfect." She looked up at him. "You're perfect."

"I'm glad you think so, lass, but this won't be if you keep looking at me like that."

Before she could ask him what he meant, he leaned down and started kissing her again. She quickly discovered that having her hands on that spectacular bare chest was even better than admiring it from afar—much better.

His skin was warm and smooth under her hands, his muscles even harder than she imagined. She loved the way they flexed instinctively under her palms when her palms squeezed or when fingers dug in every time his tongue licked deeper and deeper into her mouth.

She had that frantic, hot feeling again, and it was even worse this time with the solid weight of him on top of her. It made her forget to protest when he loosened the ties of her chemise and she felt the cool air wash over her bare skin.

She did moan, however, when his mouth found the turgid tip of her nipple. She did more than moan when he sucked. The sensation of his warm, wet mouth on her fiery, sensitive skin was too much to contain. Her entire body seemed to come off the bed as she arched and made a deep sound of pleasure. Pleasure that only intensified as she felt his tongue circling and his teeth gently tugging before the sweet suction that sent needles of pleasure to the warm, melty place between her legs.

She wanted him to touch her there again. And he did. Softly at first, with gentle, deft sweeps of his finger against her damp, tender flesh, and then when her hips started to lift and beg, with the friction and stroking her body had already learned to desire.

She could feel his own urgency racing along with hers as the soft gasps of her increasing pleasure mingled with the tight, contained groans of his.

He was holding himself back. He wanted something from her first.

Izzie knew what it was. She wanted to say she let go and allowed the sensations to break over her, but she knew who was in control. She'd given him her body, and she only hoped in doing so that he would want her heart along with it.

RANDOLPH'S CHEST SQUEEZED AS HE heard the soft cries of her release as the flush of pleasure swept over her angelic face. He was concentrating so intently on not joining her that it took him a moment to realize the stab—of conscience. This was wrong. She was a maid, and he'd never divested a lass of her maidenhead before. For good reason. It was dishonorable. A sin. She deserved a ring and a marriage bed. *His* ring and marriage bed.

But she'd refused him.

Of course she hadn't really meant it, he told himself. This would only hasten the inevitable.

Besides, it was too late. He didn't think he could stop now if he wanted to. And he sure as hell didn't want to. Just looking at her made his chest squeeze with a longing so intense it crushed the momentary flicker of doubt. He wanted this woman more than he'd ever wanted a woman before—which might have concerned him if he'd thought about it. But he wasn't going to think about it. Something about this simply felt right, and despite the lust pounding at the base of his spine, an odd calmness came over him as he untied his breeches and wrapped his hand around his cock to guide himself inside her.

He didn't need to give himself the usual perfunctory stroke to make sure he was ready; he was as hard as a rock and too close to release as it was.

Which also surprised him. Of late, he'd felt a sense of boredom—of sameness—in his interludes with women that had led to increasingly adventuresome bed sport to make it a little more interesting and exciting.

But right now he wasn't even sure he'd be able to last long in the most basic and conventional position. He couldn't imagine taking her from behind, having her on top of him, or having her mouth on him while he had his tongue…

Ah hell, not the thing to think about right now. Later. But maybe that wasn't a good idea. The lass was driving him mad with lust as it was—heaven knew the kind of havoc she could wreak if she learned of the intimate power she could wield over him.

He might never want to leave her bed.

He frowned at the thought, but it fell away the moment he looked down at her. His chest tightened again. She was so beautiful like this. Warm and soft and achingly ready for him, her cheeks still flushed and her eyes still half-lidded from her release. He didn't think he'd ever seen anything more beautiful.

Unable to hold back another minute, he nudged the head of his cock against the slick folds of her opening and groaned.

God, that felt good. He couldn't wait to be inside her.

Her eyes flew open at contact. Reading the maidenly shock and sudden uncertainty in her big blue eyes, he knew she needed reassurance. "It will be all right, *mo ghrá*. I will make it good for you—trust me."

But as soon as he uttered the words, he felt a powerful urge to take them back. *Could* he make it good for her? He'd never had a problem before, but Izzie was different.

Different. The word resonated, but he didn't want to listen. It was that she was a virgin—that was all—and from everything he'd heard, it was painful for women the first time. His first time he'd thought he'd died and gone to heaven.

But what if she didn't feel the same? He wanted her to feel the same. It was imperative that she felt the same. She *had* to feel the same, damn it.

Suddenly the size of the erection in his hand that always elicited widened eyes and gasps of excited surprise from his experienced bed-partners felt like a detriment. Was he too big? Would he hurt her more than necessary? For the first time in his life, Randolph wished he was more modestly proportioned. For a man who didn't have a modest bone in his body, it was a jarring thought.

Bloody hell, this was not the time for self-doubt. The fact that he had it was bad enough. He was experienced. He'd done practically everything (everything that interested him anyway). But it only grew worse when she nodded, her lovely heavily lashed eyes wide with trust. Randolph gritted his teeth, vowing to do whatever it took to deserve that trust.

Even if it killed him.

Slowly, with a gentle little circle of his hips, he started to push inside. Instinctively, she tightened, her body fighting the intrusion, while at the same time, the soft dampness of her body tempted him to go deeper and faster—God, it tempted—but he forced himself to go slow.

He was rewarded when he felt her relax, and the muscles fighting him start to open. His arms were taut as he held himself rigidly over her. Actually most of the muscles in his body were taut as he fought to contain the desire—the need—to thrust.

Blood pumped through his veins, and his heart pounded in his ears with the primitive urge to sink in deep and hard. To end the torture.

But he held tight. His teeth clenched and his body slickening with heat as he concentrated all his effort on making her feel good. Because God knew he felt bloody incredible.

She must be feeling pretty good, too, because with each little stroke, her cheeks were turning a little more pink and her gasps were getting a little louder—and more insistent.

She was so tight... gripping him... Sweat from the effort to hold back started to bead on his forehead.

There was only so much gentling he could do before reaching the point of no return, the final nudge that would breach the divide between maid and woman. *His* woman.

She seemed to know it was time, too. Her gaze locked on his, looking for something. Assurance? Answers? Meaning? Promises?

He was surprised at that moment how much he wanted to give them to her. But as always with her, he couldn't find the words—even when he might want them.

Instead, he shifted his weight to one arm to bring her hand to his mouth. His chest filled with a strange heat. A warmth. A feeling of contentment that seemed to brim over.

She seemed just as surprised as he by the courtly gesture in the midst of what otherwise might seem illicit. "I don't want to hurt you," he said softly, "but it will—for a moment."

At least he hoped it was only a moment.

She nodded, although clearly from the twinge of trepidation that crossed her face, she didn't fully believe him.

Perhaps his honor had not completely deserted him. Somehow he found the strength to ask, "Are you sure?"

"I have never been more sure of anything in my life. Show me. Please, show me."

The soft plea was uttered with such urgency, Randolph could only answer with a groan of relief and a final thrust of possession.

Isabel Stewart had given herself to him, and he would never give her back.

IZZIE CRED OUT—ACTUALLY IT might have been more of a scream—at the shock of pain. Even with the warning, the biting sharpness had been unexpected.

But good gracious, she felt as if she'd been split in two.

The quick glance she'd stolen of his manhood before he started to press inside her had alerted her to the problem. But she thought he would realize that he was too large to fit. He'd almost convinced her that it might work—right up to the last moment. Now she just wanted him off—and out—of her.

She started to push against that powerful chest that she partially blamed for her predicament. If he wasn't so incredible to look at, she wouldn't have been so aroused in the first place.

He swore and grabbed her wrists, pushing them back on either side of her head. She struggled for about a second before realizing she would have more chance of bending steel. Stretched out under him like this, she felt protected and vulnerable at the same time. But despite the pain he'd just given her, she knew he wouldn't hurt her.

"I'm sorry, love. Just give it a moment."

Love. It was the second time he'd called her that. *Mo ghrá*—my love. Did he even realize it?

Her heart squeezed with longing that stole her breath. She told herself not to put too much store in it, but coupled with the infinite tenderness of his lovemaking (up until that painful part), she wanted to think this meant something to him, too.

To her it meant everything.

She looked at the handsome face poised inches over hers and stared deep into his eyes, searching for answers.

She must have found them because she realized it didn't hurt so much anymore. Suddenly, she was conscious of something else, of the fact that they were joined together. That he was inside her—filling her. Maybe filling her a little too much, but other than the sense of overwhelming fullness, he wasn't hurting her anymore. The pinching was gone. It felt wonderful... significant... powerful.

Slowly, the tension started to ease from her muscles. It eased even more when he took her silence for an invitation to kiss her. Or maybe it was to stop her from more protests. Whatever the reason, it worked, and her body relaxed even more.

It more than relaxed. She started to feel the now unmistakable twinges of arousal. Was it only two weeks ago that she'd really been kissed for the first time, and now she had a wanton's understanding of her body? Good grief, what had he done to her?

Maybe she didn't know everything. When he finally started to move, slowly sliding himself in and out of her, she was at a loss. Was she supposed to do something? God knew what he was doing to her felt incredible, but what about him? If the tortured look of barely repressed ecstasy on his face was any indication, perhaps she was doing enough. She had the sense that he was struggling to hold on.

"Tell me what to do," she said softly.

"Nothing," he gritted out from between clenched teeth. "Don't move. If you move, I'm not going to last."

As she rather liked what he was doing, Izzie didn't move. She just held on.

He'd released her wrists and her hands instinctively went to his shoulders to brace herself against the jarring as his pace intensified, and the slow slides gave way to deeper and faster thrusts. She only wished that she had something to brace her heart. But their eyes held and with every stroke, her heart lifted higher and higher. She couldn't rein it in.

The tenderness of his lovemaking had shattered every last barrier of self-protection. Izzie loved him with her whole heart and told herself that she could not be alone. How could he not be feeling the same thing? He was. He had to be.

With nothing holding her back now, she gave herself over to the sensations. She let them carry her away to a place that he had shown her. To the place where sensation reached its highest peak and her body shattered.

She felt the frantic restlessness, the quickening of her pulse, and the steady building toward something that seemed tantalizingly out of reach. But this time it wasn't just her body experiencing the ecstasy, it was also her heart. For as the final rush of pleasure surged through her body, she looked into his eyes and found something that gave her hope: surprise. This was new to him. It *was* different.

She wasn't alone, and the knowledge only intensified the feelings she was experiencing. She hadn't thought she could feel anything more powerful than the first time—she was wrong. It was so much more when sharing it with the man she loved. Seeing his face transform, feeling the rush of warmth inside her, knowing that he was experiencing the same pleasure as her... that wasn't just touching heaven, it was heaven.

It took a long time to come back down to earth. Finally, he collapsed on top of her. The fierce pounding of his heart against hers only added to the feeling of closeness—of being one.

Randolph was so motionless, were it not for his heavy breathing, she might have thought that she'd killed him.

Was everything all right?

Apparently, it was. He muttered a blasphemy and rolled off her. In doing so, he pulled himself from her body and broke the connection between them. She felt the loss and wanted to hold on, but it was already gone.

The sudden cold shock didn't last long. He pulled her against his body, nestling her against the warmth of his chest. Despite the undoubtedly tawdry display of half pulled off clothes and tangled limbs, it felt like heaven again.

Pressing her cheek against his chest, Izzie listened as the pounding of his heart slowed and felt an almost trancelike happiness.

He broke the silence with a heavy sigh of contentment, echoing her thoughts. "I could stay like this forever."

But would he? Izzie had to know. She had to find out whether her instincts had been right. Whether he had felt the same things as she.

She turned her head, propping her chin on her hand to look up at him. The arrogantly refined, handsome features looked so relaxed—almost boyish. Her heart squeezed a little more. Like this he was hers.

"I love you," she said and waited.

She felt his heart stop for a long heartbeat before starting again. She felt like an axe was hanging over her head—or maybe her heart.

Tell me you love me, too. Tell me I wasn't wrong. Hold me in your arms and tell me you'll never let go.

She honestly thought he might, which made it more crushing when he didn't.

"I know." His eyes were cruelly understanding and tender. "You wouldn't be here if you didn't."

I know. It wasn't stated arrogantly but matter-of-factly.

Of course, it was hardly a surprise. How could she not? Everyone did. It must be something he'd heard a hundred times. *What's not to love?*

But he had no idea how much his words had hurt. How he was breaking her heart with his gentle smile.

She turned away so he wouldn't see the tears in her eyes. She didn't understand. How could he make love to her like that and not love her?

But what did she really know? She was an innocent—or had been until a few minutes ago. Maybe there was nothing different or special about what had just happened between them at all.

"We will be married as soon as the banns are read," he proclaimed matter-of-factly.

"I'm not marrying you," she said quietly, not turning her head to look at him.

His heart stopped again under her palm. It took longer to restart this time. "Of course you're going to marry me. You just gave yourself to me."

She'd given him everything, but he'd only accepted part.

"It isn't enough." She knew that now.

He repositioned her so that she was forced to look at him. He didn't look happy. "What do you mean it's not enough? It was pretty damned spectacular."

"Was it?" She shrugged as if it didn't matter to her, when it actually meant everything. "I will have to take your word for it as I have nothing in the way of comparison. But spectacular isn't enough for me."

Maybe she was the one who wanted perfect.

Making love to him had told her what she needed to know. She could never marry him without love. Passion wasn't enough. Satisfaction in the bedchamber would not make up for the fact that he didn't love her, nor would it make her heart break any less when he left her for another. She couldn't share him. She wanted to be enough.

She'd gambled her innocence and lost. Although maybe it wasn't a complete loss. At least now she knew the truth. He didn't love her, or he was determined not to—both amounted to the same thing.

She'd had enough. She was done trying to make him see. The man was blind and could stay that way for the rest of his life for all she cared. She wasn't going to waste any more heartache chasing after someone who didn't want her.

"What do you mean it's not enough?" He sounded like he was about ten years old. But she wasn't in the mood to pacify men who acted like little boys.

She sat up to make her way off the bed, but he grabbed her wrist to stop her. The handsome features that she'd admired not long ago were dark with anger and frustration. "Is this your way of trying to extract promises from me?"

She gave him a look of contempt that wasn't half of what she was feeling. "You don't know me at all. I told you before, I want nothing from you." She adjusted her dress as best she could knowing there was nothing she could do about the ties at the back. Removing her cloak from the floor, she pulled it around her shoulders. Her focus was on the door. All she wanted to do was get out of there.

He'd started to retrieve his clothes as well and was much more efficient at putting them on. When he realized that she meant to leave, he blocked her exit. "You aren't going anywhere until we settle things. You have to marry me, damn it."

His proposals just kept getting better and better. "Why? Because you took my maidenhead and honor demands it? I'm certainly not going to tell anyone, and I hardly think you will tarnish that shiny mail of yours by shouting it from the rooftops. Sir Thomas Randolph divesting virgins of their maidenhead? What would people think? Especially when they learn I've refused to marry you, too."

The reference to her cousin made his mouth press into a cold white line. "Walter will make you."

"Will he? I wouldn't be so sure. And no one can make me say vows before God. These are not the days of brigands and barbarians, my lord—women cannot be compelled to marry someone they do not want. And I do not want you. Now get out of my way."

He seemed momentarily stunned by her vehemence and let her pass. She was through the door and down the stairs before she realized he was behind her.

She was about to turn and tell him to go away, when he growled, "You aren't walking back alone."

Realizing it was useless to argue—not to mention foolhardy to walk by herself—she ignored him instead.

She was the only one to do so. On the mile-long journey down to the abbey, it seemed as though half the town of Edinburgh—still celebrating—stopped him to gush, fawn, and offer their congratulations on his miraculous taking of the castle. He spent most of that mile running afterward to catch up to her.

An enormous sense of relief came over her when the guesthouse finally came into view. She couldn't bear to look at him right then; she just wanted him gone. With nothing left to say—thank you hardly seemed appropriate under the circumstances—she started toward the door.

Before she could make her escape, however, he stopped her. He seemed to have calmed down a little and didn't look as angry. He had his charming knight smile on. Here was the part where he said whatever he thought she wanted to here. *It is all an act. Always. How can I have forgotten?*

"Wait. You can't just go like this. I didn't mean to upset you. I don't want you to overreact and make any hasty decisions. Why don't you think about it for a few days?"

"I don't need to think about anything. I've made my decision."

His jaw hardened again—this time with a furious tic. "How can you say that after what just happened? I know it was your first time, but you can't tell me you didn't enjoy it."

He actually sounded a little uncertain. She shook her head, dumbfounded. Was that what this was about? Had she wounded his masculine pride by not being overcome by his lovemaking? She had been, but not in the way he meant. "Have no fear, my lord. Your talents in the bedchamber are not exaggerated. I was properly swept away into complete euphoric bliss."

He looked so relieved that were her heart not being twisted in a vise, she might have laughed. Had she really made the vaunted rogue worry that he'd left her underwhelmed? He didn't understand at all. Why should he? For him the bedchamber was enough. To him it was everything.

"Then why...?" He finished his own question. "You want me to say it, is that it?" His voice had risen with his anger. "Fine. I love you, and I will keep my damned vows. Does that make you happy? Is that what you need to hear?"

She didn't think it possible that he could make her pity him. But the great hero of Scotland—the man who seemed to have everything—had just succeeded. And she wasn't alone. The two massive warriors who'd just come out of the king's former lodgings with some of his things heard his words as well and both men shook their heads as if they felt sorry for him.

But it wasn't just pity that she felt. Randolph had also given her the confirmation that she was doing the right thing. He didn't want her; he just didn't want her to refuse him. She looked at him without hesitation, and with remarkable composure for someone who'd just had a knife stuck in her gut. "Sir Thomas?" His gaze met hers, and even through the fury, she sensed that he knew he'd gone too far. That maybe he was a little shamefaced. "Go to hell."

She'd had enough. As soon as she could talk to Walter and arrange it, Izzie was going home. It was time to stop playacting in faerie tales and get on with her life.

CHAPTER ELEVEN

"RANDY, RANDY, RANDY." THE BIG Norseman—*half* Norseman, but all bloody pirate—shook his head. "With all that experience and supposed charm, do you know *anything* about lasses?"

"Go to hell, Hawk."

"I think you were the one directed to do that. And by the look on your face the past few days, you are there." The pain-in-his-arse seafarer and member of the king's secret fighting force known as the Highland Guard leaned back on the bench against the wall, kicked out his feet, crossed his arms, and shook his head with a broad smile on his face. "I'd nearly given up hope that I'd live to see this day. But damn if it wasn't worth the wait. For someone who didn't want to fight like a brigand, you sure as hell look like one."

Randolph squeezed the pewter goblet in his hand until it almost bent. He'd had years of practice in ignoring Hawk's jabs—including more than one about Randolph's unfortunate words to explain why he'd switched allegiance (Christ, he'd been young and pompous!)—but he'd never been closer to slamming his fist through that flashing white grin. Only the knowledge that it would make the bastard think he was right stopped him.

There was nothing wrong with him, damn it. He didn't care that he'd asked her to marry him. That she'd refused him. That she'd ridden out of the abbey two and a half days ago for Bonkyll Castle with a handful of Walter Stewart's men without a word to him. She'd just *left*!

But he didn't care, damn it. She would realize she'd made a mistake and come back soon enough. He'd give her a week. Maybe two. If she hadn't returned by then, he might just have to ride the forty miles to Bonkyll himself to hear her apology.

Until then, he'd distract himself with the beautiful serving lass who'd been keeping his goblet nice and full, and making her interest clear every time she leaned over to pour and give him a fantastic view of her very sizable breasts. Women were always a good distraction.

At least they used to be. But when he smiled encouragingly at the lass, and she leaned over to fill his goblet again, presenting her hefty bosom for closer inspection—practically right under his nose—all he could see was flawless, creamy white skin and soft round mounds with delicate pink tips that fit right in his hands and tasted like warm honey.

He bit back the curse of disgust, but the lass seemed to pick up on the change of plans. She lifted her eyes questioningly, and he shook his head. She moved off.

Izzie had ruined him, damn it! Randolph knew exactly who he had to blame for this. He was tempted to ride to Bonkyll right now and give her that opportunity to apologize right now.

"It won't work you know," the smug bastard watching him said. "Take my word for it, lad, fighting and denying it won't change a damned thing. And another lass sure as hell isn't the way—just ask MacGregor."

Randolph didn't need to ask MacGregor anything. He'd been there when the greatest archer in Scotland had been doing his penance to his now wife, who also happened to be Bruce's daughter and Randolph's kinswoman, after she'd caught him in an unfortunate situation. But this wasn't the same thing. MacGregor had been out of his mind in love with Cate.

He glanced down the table at the man reputed to be the most handsome in Scotland, who only had eyes for the dainty, dark-haired pixie seated next to him.

"It isn't the same," Randolph said.

He'd addressed Hawk but it was the seafarer's cousin, Lachlan MacRuairi, who answered. "Isn't it? From where I'm sitting it looks exactly the same."

"Why don't you take that poleaxe out of your arse for once, Randy, and just admit you love the lass," Hawk said. "One bad-tempered brigand around here is enough."

MacRuairi—the bad-tempered brigand he'd been referring to—called his cousin a vile name and told him to do something that was impossible.

"I'm not in love with her," Randolph insisted.

He felt the faces of a half-dozen Guardsmen on him. Why the hell was he sitting with them, anyway? Because his uncle had sent him away from the dais and told him not to come back until he stopped sulking.

He wasn't sulking, damn it. He just didn't feel like talking. He was the only one. It seemed half of Edinburgh had heard about his broken engagement and the one that had been refused. Strangely, he didn't give a shite. His pride should be stinging, but instead it was his chest that hurt. Ever since that night when she'd walked away, it had felt as if it was burning. He would have to see Helen MacKay if it didn't go away soon.

"How are you so sure?" MacRuairi asked.

"She irritates me too much."

Hawk laughed—as did a few of the others. Even MacRuairi seemed to be smiling, but with him it was always hard to be sure.

Randolph looked around at them and felt his temper spark. It reminded him of when he'd been in school. It was that sense that everyone around him understood except for him.

Magnus MacKay exchanged a look with his brother-in-law Kenneth Sutherland, and then very slowly—not unlike Randolph's teachers had done—said, "Any other woman ever irritate you like she does?"

"Hell no!" Randolph responded vehemently. "Not even close."

The men around him waited for him to catch up. He was incredulous when he realized what they meant. "So that's what love is? Irritation?"

That was absurd.

The men around him shrugged. "Sometimes," Hawk said. "Especially at first."

Christ, they were serious. "Why the hell didn't someone tell me?"

"It's one of those secrets lasses like to keep to themselves." MacSorley paused, giving Randolph a look of sympathy. "I'm sorry to say, there's a lot of them—and you are supposed to instinctively know all of them."

Randolph swore. He thought back through the list of signs that he'd identified to tell whether someone was in love and felt the noose of inevitability tightening around his neck. He was doomed, damn it. Doomed. Pretty soon he'd be wearing that idiot smile with a handful of children sitting on his lap—and pups!

God, it was already happening. He could feel his mouth curving right now!

"This was a mistake, damn it!" he said, slamming his goblet down. "I told her I had no intention of falling in love with her."

Was there such a thing as a collective wince? If there was, he'd just seen it.

"You didn't?" Hawk said.

Randolph nodded and the look of sympathy from the big seafarers face alarmed him.

"I don't envy you, Randy," Hawk said. "I hope you know how to grovel."

"You can always teach him," MacRuairi said.

"I didn't grovel," Hawk snapped.

"That's not what I hear from Ellie and Domnall," MacRuairi shot back.

But Randolph was too worried to enjoy Hawk being the one prodded. He told himself not to worry. "Izzie isn't like that. She will listen to reason."

He would apologize for his ignorance, tell her that he

loved her, and everything would be all right.

"I hope you're right," Hawk said. "But if you aren't, you can always do what I did and abduct her. Take my word for it, lasses find it romantic."

"Abduct her? Are you mad? I'm not a brigand."

Randolph ignored Hawk's "we'll see" smile as there was a commotion at the dais. He could see Walter Stewart frantically talking to the king.

"Wonder what that's about," MacKay said.

Randolph intended to find out. He arrived just in time to hear his uncle say, "Take whomever you need. I hope there is another explanation."

Walter shook his head. "I don't think so. Izzie came to live with Douglas because she expected something like this. We all just thought he'd given up. Alexander said he would conscript Langton to help find her—he will have even more reason to find her once my message arrives that she has agreed to marry him."

Randolph's heart had stopped at the mention of Izzie, but at the words "marry him," he knew that he must have been mistaken.

"What is going on here?" he asked in a far calmer voice than he would have otherwise.

Young Walter turned and looked at him with a very worried look on his face. "It's my cousin, Isabel." Not realizing his words had stopped Randolph's heart again, he continued. "She still hasn't arrived at Bonkyll. The message I sent ahead of her to her brother got there, but she and the men I sent with her are missing."

Missing? Randolph felt as if every drop of blood had drained from his body. "What do you mean missing? She left two and a half days ago. She should have arrived yesterday."

Randolph was too agitated to pay mind to the look of confusion on Walter's face. The lad must be the only one in Edinburgh who hadn't heard about Randolph's rejected proposal.

"There was some trouble a few months back," Walter

explained.

Randolph felt like he was trying to contain a volcano that was about to explode within him. "Trouble? What kind of trouble?"

Walter explained about the young knight who'd tried to erase his debts by marrying her and hadn't been pleased to have his plans foiled. "He's an unscrupulous sort," Walter added. "Alexander—Izzie's eldest brother—had broken with him some time ago, but Izzie didn't know when she became, um, involved with him."

How could no one have told him, damn it? The thought of her in danger made everything inside him turn upside down. It shattered whatever last doubts he might have had about his true feelings. He tried to stay calm, but inside he was a mad rush of twisting, terrifying emotions—foremost among them panic. "And you think he is the reason she has not arrived?"

Walter nodded. "I hope not, but it seems likely."

"I'll kill him." Randolph's voice left no doubt that he meant it. "I'll find her," he told Walter. To his uncle, he added, "I'm taking Lamont." It wasn't a question, but Bruce nodded as if it had been. Ewen "Hunter" Lamont was the best tracker in the Highlands. If anyone could find her, he could.

I will find her, damn it.

"That is gracious of you to offer, Randolph, but it isn't necessary. I can—"

Randolph took the lad by the arm and held him up almost off the ground. "I'm going."

Wisely, Walter just nodded.

Randolph started to move off before something niggled. He turned back. "You mentioned a betrothal."

"Aye. With Sir William de Vipont, Lord of Langton. She told me to accept him right before she left. I just sent the missive yesterday."

It was strange how a body that was burning could turn instantly to ice. She'd agreed to marry someone else? Randolph's chest twisted for one long painful moment

before he turned to his uncle. "I'll need MacRuairi, too."
The former pirate was nearly as good at tracking as Lamont,
and despite being from the Isles, he was one of their best
riders. Then he explained to a clearly confused Walter, "She
isn't going to marry him."

Walter frowned. "Yes, she is."

"No, she's not. She's going to marry me."

Randolph didn't realize Hawk had come up behind him.
He could practically hear the bastard laughing. "I thought
the lass rejected you, Randy."

Keenly aware that everyone in the Great Hall was
watching, Randolph spoke loudly so that they would all
hear. "She has to marry me. I ravished her, and I have every
bloody intention of doing so again when I find her."

The shocked hush that descended over the Hall was
almost comical. The reputation that Randolph had so
carefully built since his return to his uncle's fold had just
been shattered.

But for the first time in eight years, Hawk smiled and
gave him a nod of unmistakable approval.

IZZIE DIDN'T DIE OF HEARTBREAK. Although for a few days
it felt as if she might. By the time Walter had arranged for
men to escort her home, she was glad to leave Edinburgh
Castle—and Sir Thomas Randolph—behind. His angry
declaration of love had been the final nail through her heart.
That he could utter the words she so longed to hear as if
they meant nothing and with such obvious insincerity was
proof of his lack of feeling. He would tell her whatever she
wanted to hear to prevent her from refusing him and save
his pride and reputation.

Still, she wouldn't have embarrassed him by making her
refusal public. She'd said nothing of the incident, but the
men who'd overheard their argument had obviously not
been so closemouthed. It had been the talk of Edinburgh—
which is also why she'd left. She grew tired of the stares

and whispers and hoped that with her gone, the talk would die down.

"That is the woman who refused Randolph?"

With Elizabeth having run off after Thomas MacGowan, who'd left the same night that she and Randolph had made... She shook off the memory. Joanna had been the one she confided in. Izzie knew that Joanna's advice to be patient—that Randolph would figure it out—was kindly meant, but Joanna hadn't been there. It was too late. He'd hurt her too badly and proved to her that he would never be able to give her what she wanted.

As much as she loved him, Izzie knew it would be infinitely worse to be married to him and forced to confront that unrequited love every day for the rest of her life. She'd been right in the beginning. Respect, loyalty, and affection were the most she could hope for in a marriage—to want anything more was impractical and would only lead to heartache. She would have that kind of marriage with Sir William, and with no reason to refuse him, she told Walter to send her acceptance before she'd ridden out with the handful of men he'd conscripted to escort her.

If her heart had ached and she'd had to force herself not to look back over her shoulder at the castle on the rock that would make Randolph a legend, she told herself it would get easier.

It did for a while. Of course that was because she'd been abducted. When Stephen Dunbar—she refused to refer to him as "Sir" after his barbarous actions—surrounded her handful of men with a dozen of his own, and she'd guessed his intention, she'd been too terrified to think of anything but how she was going to escape. Well, maybe that wasn't exactly true. She might have experienced a heart-clenching moment of wishing Randolph was there before pushing it aside. The hero wasn't going to come to her rescue this time. If anyone was going to get her out of this, it was she.

Instinctively, she realized that if she tried to oppose Stephen she could very well end up raped before she was forced to wed so she had to somehow make him think it wasn't necessary.

It took her only a moment to burst into happy tears. "Thank goodness you have come! I thought you forgot all about me." She said the last almost chastisingly, as if he'd somehow let her down. Stephen looked at her as if she'd grown a second head. "We must move quickly if we are to get away before my brother becomes worried and sends men after us."

Now it wasn't just Stephen looking at her as if she was crazed—Walter's men were as well.

"How did you know how to find us?" she asked, then before Stephen could stop the whirlwind that she was spinning around them and think, she added, "Never mind. All that matters is that you are here now. Do you have a priest?"

Stephen recovered enough to shake his head and say, "Not yet."

Good grief, he was actually believing this rubbish? The louse was more arrogant than she'd realized. Or perhaps Randolph wasn't the only one who knew how to playact. Her heart squeezed, but she couldn't think of him now.

She put her hand to her chin as if deep in thought. "I believe I can think of one, but perhaps it would be best if you let my men go first. They will only slow us down, and it would be better if they do not hear our plans."

She may have gone a little far. His eyes narrowed. "They will go straight to your brother."

She pretended not to have thought about that. "You are quite right. Good idea. You will just have to tie them up."

The captain of the guard who'd accompanied her started to object, but Izzie was trying to avoid bloodshed and knew it would be easier for her to get away on her own. Walter's men were outnumbered at least two to one, and she feared if they came with her they would try something gallant. She also didn't want Stephen to simply try to kill them now.

Fortunately, he went along with her plan as if it had been his own. He ordered his men to tie them up, and a short while later they were riding away. Hiding her fear and pretending to be happy as they left the men behind was one of the hardest things she'd ever done. But she did it, and it paid off later when she had her chance to escape.

Stephen had gone into the church she'd picked near the coast to speak with the priest. She asked for a moment of privacy. She wasn't surprised when one of his men insisted on going with her, but the moment he turned his back, she slipped away.

She'd chosen this church for a reason. As a child, her father had brought her and her brothers to this beach to explore the caves in the sea cliffs. They could be dangerous, depending on the tide, but fortune was with her—at least at first. From her refuge in one of the caves, she heard Stephen and his men riding up and down the beach and surrounding area looking for her all through the night. His tenacity surprised her. It also nearly killed her when the tide came in.

She'd spent most of the next morning huddled on a rock high in the back of the cave that was largely hidden from site from the beach, hoping that she didn't have to try to swim her way out. By time the tide receded, it was already midafternoon. She took refuge in the church with the very kind priest who'd been forced to deal with the irate knight the day before—she apologized for that—ate some porridge and bread and accepted his offer of lodging for the night. The following morning he rode her to Bonkyll castle on the back of his very old mare with her hidden under a friar's brown hooded robe that seemed to have more moth holes than cloth left.

But the disguise proved unnecessary, as they didn't cross paths with Stephen Dunbar again. Her adventure was over late that afternoon when they passed through the familiar yett of Bonkyll Castle. She wasn't surprised to hear from one of the guardsmen left behind that her brother and most of his men had ridden out in search of her when she hadn't arrived as expected. She was relieved, however, to hear that Walter's tied up men had been found and were part of the search party.

All Izzie wanted to do was take a bath and collapse in

her own bed. She'd accomplished the first part and was walking across the yard with still-damp hair, from the kitchen toward the donjon tower, eager to crawl between those clean bed sheets, when the cry went out that riders were approaching.

At first she thought it was her brother. It was, but Alexander wasn't alone. There were at least two score of men, including... Her heart stilled as she saw the familiar red and gold arms of at least a dozen of the men. A moment later their dirty, dusty, and very rumpled-looking leader came into view.

Randolph.

Just the name made her heart skitter. He looked so unlike himself—so disreputable and unkempt—that were he not wearing his surcoat, she might not have recognized the grizzled, fierce-looking warrior as the famous knight. She turned away before their eyes could meet, knowing she was too raw and emotional from her ordeal to face him right now. Why was he here? Some ridiculous sense of duty upon hearing that she was missing?

Why couldn't he just leave her alone? Did he need to make this so hard?

She turned to address her brother, who was dismounting when she was lifted off the ground and spun around into a familiar pair of steely arms. He crushed her to his chest and buried his face in her damp hair as if he could drink her in. Despite the coldness in her heart, her body wasn't immune and warmed instantly.

"Thank God, you are all right. I feared the worst when we caught up with Dunbar and you weren't with him. Christ, you scared me. What the hell happened? Where did you go?"

Stiffly, she extracted herself from his arms. It didn't hurt as much as she expected. She felt surprisingly hollow. "I'm afraid you rode here for nothing, my lord. I managed to facilitate my own rescue. Your services were not needed."

She'd never wanted the hero—only the man.

He frowned at her cool, passionless tone. What had he

expected? That she would fall to her knees with gratitude to see him?

"Sir Harold"—the leader of Walter's guard—"said that you went with them willingly?" her brother asked.

"Aye," she nodded. "I wanted to disarm him—to think that I was happy to see him so he wouldn't watch me so closely or... do something rash."

They all knew what she meant by rash. She thought Randolph made a sound like a growl, but she didn't want to look at him. Sensing that he might reach for her again, she put a few more steps of distance between them. She gave a brief, concise explanation of the rest, neglecting to mention the perilous tide and long night in the cave.

"That was quick thinking, lass," a big, powerfully built warrior who'd ridden in behind Randolph said. He wore a nasal helm like a few of the others, but had pulled it off to reveal blond hair, blue eyes, and an extremely handsome face. She'd seen him with the king before. Erik MacSorley, she thought his name to be—a West Highland Chieftain who had been with the king from the beginning.

"Apparently, I'm not a bad actor," she said, returning his smile and ignoring the stiffening of the man who wouldn't seem to leave her side. She finished her story. "The priest rode me back a short while ago, and fortunately we did not cross paths with Sir Stephen."

"Fortune had nothing to do with it," Randolph said in a flat voice that made her turn to look at him questioningly. "He has been taken care of."

"How?"

Though one side of his mouth curved up, his expression made her shiver. "Suffice it to say that he won't be bothering you again."

Though she had no feelings for Stephen after everything that had happened, she couldn't help but feel sorry for him. Whatever had happened, if Randolph's expression was any indication, she would probably rather not know. As he was acting rather possessive for someone who had been refused, she thought it might be best to make things clear. She turned to her brother and looked over at the men behind him. "Is Sir William with you. I thought he might be here by now?"

It wasn't her brother who answered, but Randolph. "He won't be coming."

Tired and feeling understandingly vulnerable given the past two days, Izzie lost her patience. "As he is my *betrothed*," she snapped. "I suspect he shall be."

His expression darkened. "You are not betrothed." He pulled a folded piece of parchment from his sleeve and held it up.

She gasped, realizing it must be the missive Walter had sent. A missive Randolph had obviously intercepted. "You have no right!"

"I have every right." Apparently, deciding his moment of restraint was over, he pulled her into his arms again. "The only man you are going to marry is me."

His matter-of-fact tone sparked her temper. "I believe I already refused you."

"Aye, but that was before I realized I loved you. Before I realized that I'd made the biggest mistake of my life in letting you go. I do love you, Izzie. I mean it this time."

She stared at him in disbelief. Was he for real or was this another one of his acts? Did it even matter? No, she answered herself. It didn't.

Aware that about forty faces were staring at them right now, she carefully extracted herself from his embrace once again and said in a soft voice. "As do I when I tell you that nothing you could say would compel me to marry you."

Surprisingly, rather than look at her, Randolph looked to the blond-haired warrior, MacSorley, who just shrugged. "Told you so, Randy."

"Randy?" she asked, surprised. She couldn't believe anyone would dare call the great Sir Thomas Randolph, Earl of Moray, by a diminutive.

Randolph ignored her question and shook his head. "I hope you're right," he said to the man.

What happened next was so shocking, Izzie had to blink a few times to make sure she wasn't imagining what was going on. By then she was already seated on Randolph's enormous warhorse, having been lifted very unceremoniously off her feet and plopped on top. "What are you doing?" she demanded

He didn't answer. Motioning toward his men, he mounted up behind her and they started to ride off through the gate.

"Wait!" her brother shouted—like her, obviously catching up to what was happened rather late. "Where are you taking her?"

"To one of my castles until she agrees to marry me."

"You are what?" she exclaimed, spinning around to look at him as if he were a madman—which clearly he was. "You can't abduct me!"

He looked around. Clearly, no one was making a move to stop him. "And yet I am."

She knew how to put a stop to this nonsense. "You can't do this. It will ruin your reputation."

"Too late."

"How can it be too late?"

"I already told your cousin that I ravished you."

"You did what?" She stared at him incredulously. "And Jamie didn't kill you?"

"I'd like to see him try. But not that cousin. I meant Walter. Although I'm sure Douglas has heard it by now. I did announce it to the entire castle."

That stunned her into silence. He seemed not to mind. He pulled her back against his chest, and soon the gentle swaying, warmth, and overwhelming feeling of being safe again were too much to resist. A bed and clean sheets couldn't compare. Her eyes fluttered a few times, fighting it, but eventually she gave up and fell into an exhausted—and very deep—sleep.

CHAPTER TWELVE

RANDOLPH WAS BEGINNING TO SUSPECT that Hawk was either wrong or had played one of his jests on him. Over the three days it took for them to reach his newest castle in the Highlands, which was part of the old Lordship of Buchan, Izzie hadn't given any indication that she thought his abduction romantic. She'd been deaf to his apologies and seemed to have no reaction to his declaration of love, no matter how many times he'd told her (he'd lost count). She hadn't softened toward him one bit. If anything, the stubborn lass had only dug in her heels even more.

By the time they'd arrived at Lochindorb Castle, Randolph's patience had worn thin. He'd ridden hundreds of miles, hadn't slept more than a dozen hours since he'd learned she was missing, and had spent every minute of the long hours they'd searched for her scared out of his mind. When one of his men had seen what looked to be a body with light hair floating in the sea—it turned out to be kelp—he'd actually been ill. But Izzie acted as if it—as if *he*—meant nothing. What the Devil did he have to do to convince her? She couldn't have fallen out of love with him that fast… could she?

His heart sank. She'd fallen *in* love with him quickly, what's not to say the opposite couldn't be true as well? He'd hurt her. Badly, as he was coming to realize. He'd made her think not only that she wasn't important to him, but that he thought she wasn't good enough for him. Which was patently ridiculous. She complemented him in every way that mattered. She reminded him not to take himself so seriously, to find pleasure in life, and to relax. She grounded him. She stood up to him. She'd seen through him from the start, and with her he'd never had to play a part.

But by refusing to break the betrothal with Elizabeth, Izzie thought that made her second choice. She wasn't—it had been his word he was thinking about—but she didn't see it that way.

He'd been given a chance to prove how much she'd meant to him after they'd made love, but he'd been so sure that he could control his own feelings—that he was immune to them—he didn't recognize them when they were practically banging him over the head. It had not only felt different, it *had been* different. He thought he'd experienced everything there was to experience in the bedchamber, but he realized he'd been missing out on the only thing that mattered: making love to someone you loved. It hadn't been just his body finding pleasure, it had been his soul as well. Ironically, he'd thought she would see the truth when they made love, but instead it had been him.

He could see it clearly now, but Izzie didn't seem to believe anything he said. Worse, she didn't seem all that interested. She was acting as if it were too late. As if she didn't care how he felt. But that couldn't possibly be true... could it? Nay. He wasn't going to give up until he convinced her—even if he suspected that more than once in the next few days he was just going to want to lock her in the tower and ravish her senseless until she agreed.

Thanks to her, he had a new nickname from Hawk—Brigand—and apparently it fit.

The long ride with her bottom pressing against his cock—he wasn't going to give her the chance to escape—certainly wasn't helping his newly formed barbarian instincts any. He'd been pushed to the edge by both her indifference to his apologies and the constant friction of a very soft bottom. How the lass could rouse his temper and his cock to such extraordinary lengths at the same time, he didn't know.

It was a relief when they finally reached the ferry to make the short crossing to the castle. Once on the small island, she looked around, her eyes skimming with disbelief over the burned-out outbuildings and more than half slighted walls.

She spun on him angrily. "*This* horrible pile of stones belongs to you?" She paused to add sarcastically. "Do you by chance have a castle that actually has a roof on it?"

"It has a roof." Although he wasn't sure how effective it was. The English had done a pretty thorough job of razing everything made out of wood. The stone hadn't fared much better. "I thought you would want to see the best. It will be my gift to you when you agree to marry me."

She gaped at him as if he were mad. "If this is your best castle, Randy"—he might have to kill Hawk the next time he saw him for calling him that in front of her—"then I wonder about your reputation as one of your uncle's most important knights. I also wonder about those reputed charm skills if you think to lure me to marriage with the promise of this ruin."

"I didn't say it was my best castle. I said it was the best—for you."

Now she didn't just look outraged, she also looked offended. "So I am worthy of a burned-out, slighted ruin?"

She was irritating him again. He had to clench his jaw to bite back the flare of temper. He was tempted to let her figure it out herself. "You are worthy of every great palace in the world. But I did not think it was fine towers, gold plate, velvet furnishings, and high ramparts that would please you. I love you, Izzie, and I thought this would show you how much."

When she wasn't busy driving him crazy, she was a clever lass—her quick wit and intelligence were two of the reasons he loved her—it didn't take her long to figure it out. If he hadn't been watching her so closely, he wouldn't have seen the quick intake of breath and the swell of emotion sweep over her features. "You want me to help you rebuild it?"

The gesture had touched her. For a moment the look in her eyes even gave him hope. It was as if she were a child receiving a gift for the first time.

"It will be yours. You can rebuild it how you want. If you wish me to help, I should love to, but the decisions will be yours."

She didn't say anything right away. But after a minute, she composed herself and wrestled her emotions back under firm control. "I was wrong," she said. "You deserve every bit of your reputation for charming women. But it isn't going to work." She lifted her chin, her eyes glinting with steel. "You will not bribe me into marriage."

That wasn't what he was doing, damn it. He just wanted to do something that would be meaningful to show her how much she meant to him. He took a threatening step toward her, the tension between them wound so tight he could practically feel it pulsing. Or maybe that was another part of him, damn it. "Perhaps I could think of another way. I did promise your cousin to ravish you again the next time I saw you."

The flush that rose to her cheeks told him she was not as immune to the threat as she wanted to be. She lifted her eyes defiantly to his. "You wouldn't dare."

"I wouldn't wager on it, love."

The tone of his voice must have impressed her. Her eyes widened a little, and she took a definitive step back. "What happened to you? You are acting like a brigand."

Christ, not her, too! Her calling him Randy was bad enough. "I fell in love, that's what happened." He paused. "I was scared out of my mind, Izzie. If he'd hurt you, it would have been my fault."

His expression and the pained sound in his voice must have penetrated. It was with some compassion that she assured him, "Don't be ridiculous. It had nothing to do with you. I should have expected something like that. I knew he would not just give up, but I'd convinced myself he had."

"Because you wanted to leave. Because I drove you away. Because you didn't think I cared about you. But I love you, Izzie."

At least she didn't roll her eyes or pretend she didn't hear him this time—which was progress, he supposed. "And so you decided to abduct me and lock me in this wreck of a tower *on an island* until I agree to marry you? This is how you intend to prove it to me?"

"It was supposed to be romantic. And you're not a prisoner. Although you might have trouble finding someone who will ferry you across."

She gave him a long look. "I wonder about you, Randy. Really, I do."

He still didn't like the nickname, but it was oddly fitting coming from her. She had a way of knocking him down a peg or two, and he conceded that maybe he might need it every now and then.

"And what am I supposed to do all day while I am not being held prisoner?"

He lifted a brow and gave her a wickedly suggestive look. "I can think of a few things."

Sadly, she didn't bite. "Not a chance."

He shrugged, not surprised but disappointed all the same. "This place is a mess. There is parchment and quills in your room—fix it." He started to walk toward the sea, needing a cool dip before he did something he regretted like lift her in his arms and carry her up those damned stairs himself. He turned just before he passed beyond the gate. "Don't make me wait too long, Izzie. I'm not a patient man by nature, and I'm liable to take matters into my own hands."

They both knew what he meant, and from the pink that darkened her cheeks, he knew the idea wasn't as offensive to her as she wanted it to be.

IZZIE KNEW WHAT IT FELT like to be a mouse. For two weeks she'd been hunted by a very wicked, very sneaky, very feral cat that seemed ready to pounce on her for the kill. She wanted to say that she was immune to his efforts to convince her that he loved her, but the truth was that the once-vaunted knight turned ravishing, abducting brigand was wearing her down. She didn't know what was more difficult to believe—that he'd abducted her or that he'd announced it (and her ravishment) to the world. He'd destroyed his perfect knight image for her, and it was hard not to think it meant something.

Every day he devised some devious method of knocking down the walls she'd erected around her heart. He'd laid siege to her battered emotions with such a powerful show of force, she had new respect for the English garrison at Edinburgh for holding out as long as they did. Sir Thomas Randolph knew how to wage a war—there was a reason he'd become one of the king's most trusted advisors—and he was putting the full force of those talents at work against her.

What chance did she have?

Every morning he joined her to break her fast, after which he planned some morning activity—from fishing in a secluded bay on one side of the island (she'd declined the offer to swim), to long walks along the seaside where they would discuss everything from the war to the future role he hoped to take in his uncle's government, to what to do after the war to prevent another English king from attempting to assert authority over Scotland, to his views on managing his own lands and farming, to his favorite stories and, of course, music.

She was entranced by it all. He shared his thoughts without moderation or calculation. He talked freely for what she suspected was a rarity for him.

After the midday meal when he wasn't training with his men (which she might have watched more than once from the bench she'd set up in what had been the garden, to read), he would tour her around the castle, telling her what had been where and pointing out different construction methods the previous builder had used. She'd tried to feign disinterest for as long as she could—about a day—and before she realized it, she was asking questions, discussing ideas, the pros and cons of existing modern castles (like Dunstaffnage and Kildrummy), and wondering whether there should be four towers or five. She'd started to sketch different ideas and knew it was only a matter of time before she showed them to him.

But, of course, the hardest part and most difficult to resist of his tactical assault against her defenses was the way he looked at her, the not-so-accidental touches and grazes, and the daily declaration of love. Every night before she retired for bed, he would stand outside her door (which was separated from his by a very thin wooden partition wall), and bid her good night with a simple "I love you."

But, of course, it wasn't simple at all. It was the most important thing in the world to her—if she could believe him.

He hadn't tried to kiss her, which was worse than if he had. She was dreaming about it, anticipating it, and—silly lustful fool that she was—hoping for it. Last night, he'd leaned down to sweep a strand of hair from her cheek, and thinking he finally meant to kiss her, she'd sucked in her breath so loudly she knew he must have heard. His eyes had fallen to her mouth, and she knew all she had to do was lean toward him and his mouth would have been on hers. She would have been in his arms again, and probably— definitely—in his bed again.

She'd lain awake most of the night cursing herself for not doing so. Her body was on fire as she remembered all the pleasure he had given her. She wanted to feel him inside her again. She wanted to skim her hands over every inch of that incredible body and feel his heart beating against hers again. She wanted to look into his eyes when he was sliding in and out of her and feel that powerful connection once more.

She wanted *him*.

The truth was that his two-week long seduction was working, and she didn't know how much longer she was going to be able to hold out. The question was whether she still wanted to. He'd broken her heart—could she trust him not to do so again? Could she believe him or was he still just saying what he thought she wanted to hear?

It was time to find out. That night when he escorted her to her door and told her he loved her, she didn't immediately turn to go inside her room. "Why should I believe you?" she asked. "How do I know you are not just saying the words because you think they are what I want to hear?"

He seemed momentarily stunned that they were finally talking about this, but quickly recovered. "I hoped the last two weeks would prove it to you. We belong together, Izzie. Surely you can see that?"

"My seeing it is not the problem."

"I was an idiot." She didn't disagree. "The signs were there but I didn't want to see them."

She arched a brow, intrigued in spite of herself. This ought to be good. "Signs?"

He nodded. "Aye, I stopped looking at other women, I became overprotective and possessive if anyone looked at you—Christ, I nearly punched a merchant for looking down your dress that day in the market—I forgot my honor by taking you to bed before we said our vows, and I was alternatively miserable and irrational, doing ridiculous things."

"You mean like abducting me?"

He frowned. "Nay. As I said, that was supposed to be romantic."

"Who told you that?"

"MacSorley."

"I think you had better find some new friends."

Randolph made a face. "It did seem a little, uh, unorthodox."

"That's an understatement." She gave him a long look. "So am I to understand that you now profess to love me because you took me to bed and didn't jump into another woman's, because you were a little worried about me and didn't appreciate when my bodice was the recipient of glances from other men?" She gave a half roll of her eyes.

"That hardly seems enough to build a life upon."

He didn't seem to appreciate the eye roll or her flippant tone. His gaze sharpened. "You are also the most irritating woman I have ever met."

He looked so wonderfully frustrated, she wondered if it might be time to have some pity on him. She couldn't fully hide her smile. "I am? Why didn't you say that in the first place."

He looked at her as if he couldn't believe it. "Christ, Hawk was right."

"Who?"

He shook his head. "It doesn't matter. Do you believe me?"

Amazingly, she did. "Let's just say I'm not completely opposed to the idea. It's quite a list."

He didn't seem to mind her sarcasm. "Just wait until I start walking around with a stupid grin on my face." He gave a brief shudder before continuing in earnest. "I know I acted unforgivably, but I am sorry. I've never fallen in love before, and I didn't realize what was happening to me until you left, and I thought I'd lost you." His expression grew pained—almost devastated. "I let you walk away thinking I didn't care about you, and I was out of my mind with regret and fear. Nothing else mattered but finding you and doing whatever it took to convince you that you are the most important person in the world to me. That I would be honored to have you by my side as my wife. That you are the first, second, third, and only choice. That I could never marry anyone else after being with you." He reached out to caress the curve of her cheek with his thumb. "You ruined me, sweetheart."

Her heart squeezed; it wasn't so cold anymore. "I think you've got it the wrong way around," she said wryly, instinctively burrowing her face deeper into his hand. "I was the ravished virgin."

He shook his head. "I found perfection. How could I ever settle for anything else?" He took a deep breath and looked down into her eyes. "Marry me, *mo ghrá*. I swear on my honor that I will never give you cause to regret it."

Her mouth twisted. "I don't know. Your honor has taken rather a severe beating of late. Now that you've sullied your reputation, I'm not so sure—I rather fancied marrying a great hero." She tilted her head. "Any more impossible castles for you to take by chance?"

Realizing she was teasing—and what it meant—his eyes warmed with happiness that filled her own heart.

"I'm afraid not," he said, his voice rough with emotion. "Now that my uncle Edward Bruce has made the truce with England over Stirling Castle, the last one has been taken."

She shrugged. "Oh well. I'm sure you will think of something."

He grinned. "I'm sure I will." He slid his arm around her waist and drew her to him. "Does that mean I'm forgiven?"

She nodded.

That was all he needed. He covered her mouth with a groan and pulled her deeper into his arms. He kissed her like a man who'd just found his life's reward. Like a man who would love her for the rest of his life. With every stroke of his tongue, with every touch and caress, he showed her exactly how much she meant to him. And a very few minutes later, when he'd divested them both of their clothing and carried her to bed, he showed her the perfection that would be theirs for a lifetime.

AUTHOR'S NOTE

Sir Thomas Randolph, Earl of Moray, and his rival James "the Black" Douglas have gone down in history as Robert the Bruce's two most vaunted and trusted commanders. Randolph is thought to have been a nephew of the king's, but the exact genealogy is not known. I went with what seems to be the favored ancestry of Randolph's mother, possibly named Isabel, being the daughter of Bruce's father, Niall's, second wife, whom Niall marries after Marjorie, Countess of Carrick—Bruce's mother—dies. In other words, Randolph is the son of Bruce's mother's half sister.

Although the taking of Edinburgh Castle in 1314 (also featured in *The Rock*) is undoubtedly Randolph's most famous feat, he has a long and illustrious career in his uncle's service, fighting along his side during the Wars of Independence—reputedly leading one of the divisions at the seminal Battle of Bannockburn (which features in *The Ghost,* the next book in the series,)—and serving the king in the important years that followed, culminating in the signing of the Declaration of Arbroath in 1320, where Randolph's signature appears prominently. Bruce also named him as regent to the young heir to the throne, David, a position that Randolph serves after the death of Bruce in 1329, for three years until his own death in 1332.

Randolph is rewarded well for his loyalty. In addition to the earldom of Moray, he is given the old Bruce lordship of Annandale, the lordship of Man, and the lordship of Badenoch to go along with his lands in Nithsdale, where he was born, and Lochaber.

Notwithstanding all his accomplishments and the faithful

years of service to his uncle, the accounts of Randolph always mention the one exception: the early years of the war where he briefly turns to fight with the English. I imagine it must have dogged him and couldn't resist using it in my story.

Randolph is reputedly taken prisoner by the English after the disastrous defeat at the Battle of Methven in 1306. I have it a little later in *The Hawk,* in February 1307, when Bruce's men are trying to avoid the English navy. Famously, Randolph is said to have explained his change of allegiance by saying that "the King made war like a brigand instead of fighting a pitched battle as a gentleman should." (Ronald McNair Scott, *Robert the Bruce: King of Scots,* Barnes & Noble Books, New York, 1993, pg. 111.) Although the words definitely have the feel of a later attributor, they sum up the overriding conflict in the Highland Guard series between the old "chivalric" fighting and my "pirate" warfare perfectly. While in England, Randolph was said to have been under the keeping of our old friend Sir Adam Gordon (*The Recruit* and *The Ghost*), and when he is captured yet again two years later—this time by the Scots—who do you think is in command? Why who else but Douglas! Irony, that.

Little is known about Randolph's wife, Isabel Stewart, the only daughter of John Stewart of Bonkyll, the patriot hero who dies fighting alongside Wallace at Falkirk, and Margaret Bonkyll. As is common with many of the people I write about, there are various spellings for the name: de Bonkyl, Boucle, Buncle, Bunkle and Bonkill. Isabel and Randolph have at least two sons, Thomas and John, but it is one of their daughters, Agnes, known as Black Agnes, Countess of Dunbar, who will become famous for her heroic defense of Dunbar Castle against an English siege in 1338.

In previous mentions of Randolph throughout the series, I used a version of his arms that I found from a number of sources (including the plaque dedicated to him on Edinburgh Castle): "Or, three cushions within a double tressure flory counter-flory Gules," that is red and gold. But interestingly, for the Bannockburn Live 700th anniversary celebration, the expert historians had Randolph's arms as red and white. I'm assuming that this was an earlier version—i.e. before Bannockburn and/or his earldom?—that I suspect is more accurate for my time period.

As always, you can find pictures and some of the places mentioned in *The Rogue* and more information on my website. www.MonicaMcCarty.com

ABOUT THE AUTHOR

Monica McCarty is the *New York Times* and *USA Today* bestselling author of twenty Scottish Historical romances and two Regency romances. Her books have won and been nominated for numerous awards, including the Romance Writers of America's RITA® & Golden Heart®, RT Book Reviews Reviewers' Choice, the Bookseller's Best, and Amazon's Best Books of the Year. Known for her "torrid chemistry" and "lush and steamy romance" as well as her "believable historical situations" (Publishers Weekly), her books have been translated and published throughout the world. Monica's interest in the Scottish clan system began in the most unlikely of places: a comparative legal history course at Stanford Law School. After a short, but enjoyable, stint practicing law, she realized that mixing a legal career with her husband's transitory career as a professional baseball player was not exactly a match made in heaven. So she "traded" in her legal briefs for Historical Romances with sexy alpha heroes. When not trekking across the moors and rocky seascapes of Scotland or England, Monica can be found in Northern California with her husband and two children.

Visit Monica's website at:
www.MonicaMcCarty.com
Find Monica on Facebook at:
https://www.facebook.com/AuthorMonicaMcCarty
Follow Monica on Twitter at:
https://twitter.com/monicamccarty
Sign up for Monica's Newsletter at:
http://monicamccarty.com/index.php

Made in the USA
Middletown, DE
16 July 2016